Zoey was seething with anger. Lara had caused this whole mess. Lara was directly responsible for Jake's misery. She was responsible for Kate's misery as well. *And* Lucas's because Lucas had to put up with Kate. It was ridiculous. When would it end? How much would Lara be allowed to get away with? It wasn't fair to anyone—least of all Jake.

"What are you thinking?" Jake asked.

"I, uh . . . nothing," she stammered. "I guess I'm just mad." She rubbed her temples, hopelessly wrestling with her thoughts. If she told Jake the truth now, she would be breaking her promise to Lucas . . .

Don't miss any of the books in
Making Out
by Katherine Applegate
from Avon Flare

MAKING OUT #18

Zoey speaks out

KATHERINE APPLEGATE

AN AVON  FLARE BOOK

AVON BOOKS, INC.
1350 Avenue of the Americas
New York, New York 10019

Copyright © 1996 by Daniel Weiss Associates, Inc.,
and Katherine Applegate
Published by arrangement with Daniel Weiss Associates, Inc.
Library of Congress Catalog Card Number: 99-94828
ISBN: 0-380-81120-0
www.avonbooks.com/chathamisland

First Avon Flare Printing: November 1999

AVON FLARE TRADEMARK REG. U.S. PAT. OFF. AND IN OTHER COUNTRIES, MARCA REGISTRADA, HECHO EN U.S.A.

Printed in the U.S.A.

WCD   10 9 8 7 6 5 4 3 2 1

Zoey speaks out

Zoey

Well, well, well . . .

Graduation is nearly upon us. And I suppose that the end of senior year is a time when we should all feel proud; a time when we can look back at all the hard work that went into making it through four years of high school.

There's nothing like the successful completion of an academic career. Right?

Hmmm. For some reason, I'm having a hard time getting the pride thing going. Maybe that's because this past year, school was pretty much the last thing on my mind. Personally speaking, I can't really seem to remember too much "hard work." I mean, when I think about everything that's happened since September, it's amazing I was able to get any work done at all, hard or otherwise.

Let's see. I broke up with my old boyfriend. I nearly lost my new boyfriend on several occasions. My parents almost got divorced. My brother had an operation that failed; I found out I have a half sister; my best friend ran away . . . and all this while I'm supposed to be thinking about applications and SAT scores?

I _should_ be proud, though, I guess. Or at least happy. After all, I got into the University of

California at Berkeley. It wasn't my first choice, but it wasn't my last, either.

Mostly I'm just confused.

California is where I've always dreamed of going to college, ever since I was little. But the reality of going there hasn't sunk in until now. In a little over four months I'll be leaving behind everyone and everything I love. Sure, I'll call and write and come home for vacations, but things won't ever be the same again. Ever. Nobody's even going to be _near_ me. It's pretty scary. Nobody's even going to be in the same time zone. In my mind, I keep going down the list of people I'll hardly ever see again. Lucas, my boyfriend, the one I'll probably miss most of all, is going to the University of Maine. Nina, my best friend, still has another year of school. <u>If</u> she ever decides to come home. Who knows how much school she'll have to make up if she doesn't get back soon?

Then there's Benjamin, who will be in New York City. But who knows about him, either? Ever since Christmas, when he found out he was going to be blind for the rest of his life, his behavior has been impossible to predict. He's been a total jerk to everyone. Well, everyone except our half sister, Lara McAvoy. And then there was his decision to dump Nina. And craziest of all, his most recent decision to <u>chase</u> Nina. How does he plan to find her? For all I know, he may be gone for good, too.

You know, come to think of it, maybe it's not so bad that I'm leaving Chatham Island. At this point it looks like there may not be that much to stick around for.

One

Zoey's eyes fluttered as she slowly came out of a deep sleep, with a dream of Lucas's good-night kiss still tingling on her lips. She sighed contentedly and rolled over in bed.

What a night, she thought. She blinked at the sunlight streaming through her dormered window. *A perfect way to end a perfect senior prom.*

Well, not *quite* perfect.

Zoey sat up in bed and stretched with a rueful grin. No, until the very moment Lucas had taken her into his arms on the dance floor, she'd been dreading the senior prom. She'd resigned herself to a totally disastrous night—on the one occasion that teenagers were supposed to remember forever, the most magical night of high school.

But in the end, it *had* been magical.

How was it that Lucas always found some way to make her forgive him?

He didn't even need to *say* anything. Zoey pursed her lips. All he needed to do was look at her with those soft brown eyes, and hold her, and bring his lips to hers. . . .

I'm pathetic, she said to herself. She hopped out of bed and slipped into a pair of sweatpants, then gathered her dark blond hair in a ponytail. It was almost funny how spineless she was. After all, Lucas had violated her trust in the most base, child-like way: He had sneaked a peek at her diary. And *then,* as if that wasn't bad enough, he had stolen a story out of her notebook and published it in *Folio,* an eight-page photocopied pamphlet distributed monthly to students and teachers at Weymouth High.

For a moment Zoey stood still. She was supposed to feel outraged, right? She tried to summon all the anger and indignation she'd initially felt—and ended up smiling instead. It was hopeless. No matter how badly they fought, she couldn't stay mad at him—

The phone started ringing.

Speak of the devil, she thought. She trotted downstairs to the kitchen. Knowing Lucas, he was probably calling to suggest that they start the day where they had left off the night before—namely in the throes of a passionate make-out session.

She grabbed the receiver off the phone on the kitchen wall in the middle of the third ring. "Hello?" she asked, her voice still hoarse from sleep.

"Zoey—what am I going to do?" Aisha Gray cried at the other end.

Zoey frowned. So much for a romantic wake-up call.

"Good morning to you, too, Eesh," Zoey said dryly. "I'm fine. Thanks for asking."

"I'm in no mood for jokes, Zo," Aisha snapped. "I need help. Now."

Zoey sighed, then slumped down at the kitchen table. "I know. Believe me, I know."

Unlike Zoey's prom, Aisha's had been an absolute catastrophe. And as far as Zoey could tell, the problem could have been easily avoided.

It all started when Aisha agreed to go to the prom with David Barnes. But then Christopher Shupe—the love of Aisha's life, the man who had asked for her hand in marriage—showed up unexpectedly on Chatham Island. So Aisha promptly asked *him* to the prom. Instead of accepting the fact that this was a terrible error in judgment, Aisha let Claire Geiger talk her into some harebrained scheme that was supposed to enable her to go to the prom with *both* of them. Needless to say, the plan had failed. Aisha's prom ended with both David and Christopher storming out.

"Well?" Aisha demanded. "Any suggestions?"

"Actually, yeah," Zoey replied. "Never follow Claire's advice again."

There was a pause, then Aisha laughed miserably. "Thanks," she mumbled. "I could have figured that one out for myself. What was I thinking?"

"You're asking *me?*" Zoey shook her head. "I have no idea what you were thinking. I tried telling you that it would never work. It was doomed from the start."

"I know, I know," Aisha moaned. "I mean, I still can't believe I did that. I can't believe I actually told David that Christopher was my *cousin.*"

Zoey fiddled with the phone cord. She couldn't believe it, either—but she didn't want to make Aisha feel any worse by agreeing with her. "Uh . . . have you heard from either of them yet?"

"Are you *kidding?* Neither of them wants anything to do with me. Not that I can blame them."

"Have you thought about calling them?" Zoey asked quietly.

"Sure, I've thought about it. I'm just not looking

8

forward to having the phone slammed down in my ear twice in one day."

Zoey sighed. "Eesh—you're going to have to make a decision. You're going to have to decide between them. The sooner the better."

Aisha laughed again—a short, bitter laugh. "Hate to tell you this, Zo, but I don't think I'm in any position to make that kind of decision anymore. Neither of them wants to talk to me, remember?"

"That may be true right now, but it's definitely not true in the long run. Trust me. I know. They're both hurt and confused right now. You've got to clear it up. You've got to tell David that Christopher is the one you really love. That way, it'll—"

"Wait a sec, Zo," Aisha interrupted. "Who said that Christopher is the one I really love?"

Zoey bit her lip. *Oops.* The truth was that Zoey *hoped* Aisha would choose Christopher. She just couldn't see it working out any other way. What Eesh had with Christopher was so perfect, so romantic. . . .

"You're just saying that because you don't like David," Aisha said.

"That's not true." It wasn't that Zoey didn't *like* David; she just didn't know him. And although she would never tell Aisha, she wasn't all that impressed with him. He was nice and funny and cute—but he was no Christopher Shupe.

"And you know what really makes me mad?" Aisha asked after a moment. She sighed loudly. "You're right."

Zoey smiled. "Look at it this way, Eesh. What you had with David was exactly like what I had with Aaron. Well, except for the fact that Aaron is a sleazebag. But it was just physical attraction. It was

9

a fling, you know what I mean? You have to make Christopher see that *he's* the one you see yourself with in the long run." She took a deep breath. "That's what I did with Lucas after the whole Aaron thing."

"Easier said than done," Aisha grumbled. "Speaking of Lucas, how did your evening end up?"

Zoey glanced up at Lucas's small house, perched on the hill above her backyard. "Oh, pretty good," she said noncommittally, trying not to think too hard about the way she'd kissed him and run her fingers through his long, unruly blond curls. "Amazingly enough, he was a perfect gentleman."

"Perfect?" Aisha asked dubiously.

Zoey started to blush. "Well . . . that's a slight exaggeration. But he didn't bring up the topic of you-know-what once."

"Hmmm," Aisha mused. "How very un-Lucas-like."

"Yeah, I mean, especially considering it was the prom. Not that he needs any incentive or anything. But isn't the prom supposed to be a prime occasion for losing your virginity?"

Aisha snorted. "I wouldn't know. I barely even shook hands with anyone, remember?"

"Come on, Eesh," Zoey said. "Things will work out. I promise."

"Maybe. I mean, *you* guys worked things out. How did you do that, anyway? I thought you were going to kill Lucas last night."

Zoey thought for a minute. How *did* they work things out? Her memory seemed to get fuzzy after that first kiss on the dance floor.

"Please don't tell me it had anything to do with

10

being elected prom king and queen," Aisha mumbled.

"Well . . . he apologized about the whole short-story thing."

"And?" Aisha prodded.

"And . . . he told me the only reason he looked through my stuff in the first place was because he wanted to know everything about me. He said he wanted to share in everything I do."

"Nice," Aisha muttered.

Zoey frowned. "What—you don't think so?"

"I mean, if I still had any semblance of a love life left, I would probably think that was really, really sweet. But right now it makes me want to barf."

Zoey laughed. "That sounds like something Nina would say."

As soon as the words were out of her mouth, a sudden emptiness filled the pit of her stomach. Aisha was silent. *That would be something Nina would say,* Zoey thought. *If she were here. If we could talk to her. If we even had the slightest idea where she was.*

After a few seconds Aisha sighed softly. "Look, I better get going," she said. "I've got to figure out a way to get out of this mess. Thanks, Zo."

"Thanks for what?" Zoey managed, but her voice was strained. A lump had lodged itself in her throat.

"Thanks for telling me what I needed to hear. I'll call you later, okay? Bye."

"Bye."

Zoey placed the phone back on the receiver. Her eyes swept the empty kitchen: the little breakfast nook, the cooking area, and the hallway to the foyer. She was all alone. Her parents were already at the

11

restaurant, getting ready for the Sunday rush. Normally Benjamin would have been here.

But the circumstances were far from normal.

Zoey shook her head. One thing was certain: She'd been wrong. This weekend wasn't nearly as perfect as she'd originally thought.

Nina Geiger realized with a start that she'd been sitting and staring at her reflection in the stained hotel-room mirror for almost an hour. She shivered, then reached for the crumpled pack of Lucky Strikes in the pocket of her fatigues. Luckily there was one left. Her habit of sucking on unlit cigarettes had kept her occupied throughout the long, sleepless night, and now dozens of them littered the floor.

I could have been killed, she said to herself yet again. She shoved the cigarette into her mouth. *I am so lucky. So lucky . . .*

Well, not *entirely* lucky. The creep who had attacked her last night had made off with her backpack. She'd wrestled free from him—but as she tried to escape he had grabbed her from behind. His hands had clamped down on the shoulder straps of the bag. Instinctively she had wriggled free, leaving him standing there with the backpack in his hands. Then she'd bolted back to the hotel as fast as she could.

That had been almost twelve hours ago. She could still hear him yelling at her: *"You little bitch!"* The thought of it made her sick. She'd been in her room ever since—wide awake and terrified. The curtains were drawn, but bright shafts of sunlight were poking through. For some reason, she was nervous to look outside.

It was nearly twelve noon. Hunger was beginning to pick at her stomach.

I've got to get out of here, she said to herself, taking one last look in the mirror. *I'm going crazy.*

Well, at least she could be happy about one thing: Panic, hunger, and sleeplessness did wonders for one's weight. For the first time in her life, she could actually see that she had cheekbones. Or maybe her cheekbones just looked more pronounced because her dark skin was so drawn and haggard. Black circles ringed her gray eyes. The red hair dye she had used on the way back from Miami had faded, leaving her hair in its natural state: black and sticking out in all directions.

Without thinking, she felt for her wallet. Her cash supply was rapidly dwindling, but she had her father's credit cards. *And* his permission to use them.

Suddenly a pang of guilt shot through her. What right did she have to run up a tab on her father's credit cards?

I'll make it up to him when I get home, she promised herself. *But I'm not ready to go back just yet. The only thing I'm sure of is that I have to get the hell out of Portsmouth.*

After a few more deep drags on the cigarette, she finally forced herself to stand. Her mind was made up. She would go have one last meal at Niko's—the outdoor café owned by that nice middle-aged Greek guy—then hop the next bus out of town.

The sunlight made her squint as she left the inn and walked the two blocks to the restaurant, but she was beginning to feel better. It was a beautiful spring day. A cool breeze was blowing. The smell in

13

the air reminded her of summer and the end of school. For a brief moment her thoughts turned to Chatham Island, but she quickly forced those thoughts aside. She was free now—and more important, she was safe. She should enjoy it.

"Hey, Nina!" Niko sang out from behind the counter when she walked in. He rubbed his hands on his apron and peered at her closely. "Hey—you all right? You don't look so hot."

"I'm fine," she said dismissively, sitting down on a stool. "Just hungry." She forced a tired grin. "I'll have the usual."

He hesitated. "You sure you're all right?"

She nodded, averting her eyes. "A little tired, that's all. And starved."

"Well . . . okay." He straightened and patted his paunch. "But remember, man cannot live on gyros alone—or woman, for that matter." He winked at her. "You don't want to wind up looking like me, do you?"

"I like the way you look," she said as brightly as she could manage. "Anyway, this is the last gyro I'll be having for a while. I'm leaving Portsmouth today."

"Oh, yeah?" He busied himself with preparing her food. "That's too bad. I'm gonna miss you, Nina. You're my best customer."

Nina smiled. "I'm gonna miss you, too."

"So, where are you going?" he asked.

Good question. I have no idea. "Uh . . . Boston," she said, naming the first place that popped into her head.

"No kidding," he said. He put the gyro in front of her, and she instantly began to devour it. "My brother lives in Boston. He's in the restaurant business, too. You should look him up. Where are you gonna be staying?"

"Mm-mmm." Her mouth was full. She shrugged.

Niko smiled. "Wow, kid—you really *are* hungry."

She forced herself to swallow, then took a deep breath. "I guess so," she managed.

For a moment Niko just looked at her. A thoughtful, concerned expression formed on his dark, craggy face. "Nina, do you mind if I ask you a question?" he said.

Uh-oh. Nina quickly shoved the gyro back into her mouth.

"You don't have to answer me if you don't want to," he continued quickly. "But I was just wondering . . . does your family know that you're here in Portsmouth?"

She chewed slowly, afraid to look him in the eye. She'd been worried about something like this. Now he would get all freaked out that she was a runaway, and he would probably insist that she stay put until he called the police or the orphanage—or until Mr. Geiger came all the way out to Portsmouth to get her.

"They know I'm safe," she said simply.

He nodded, then let out a deep sigh. "Okay, Nina. Just take care of yourself, okay? You're a nice kid. I've got a daughter myself, you know. She's a little younger than you. I couldn't stand it if I didn't know she was okay."

Nina crammed the last of the food into her mouth. Why was he telling her this? What was his point? She blinked rapidly, feeling a sudden wetness in her eyes. Oh, great. She was *not* going to start bawling in front of Niko and make a total fool of herself. Anyway, her father knew she was okay; that was all that mattered.

She reached into her pocket for her wallet, but Niko gently put his hand on her shoulder. "This one's on the house, Nina," he said.

She looked up at him. Her lips trembled. If she opened her mouth, she knew she would start crying. Why was he being so nice to her? Couldn't he see that he was just making her miserable?

"Just think of it as a little token of thanks for being such a great customer," he said with a wry, easygoing grin. "And promise me you'll take care of yourself, okay?" He patted her arm and turned back to the stove.

For an instant Nina paused. Then she leaped off the stool and dashed out of the restaurant, afraid that Niko would see the tears that had already started to stream down her cheeks.

LUCAS

I'm just thankful I'll
be graduating on time. I
can't believe it. It's a
miracle, actually. Half of
my high-school career was
spent in a juvenile correc-
tional facility. I mean,
it's sort of hard to imagine
that credits earned in
Youth Authority would
really transfer to Wey-
mouth High. Most of the kids
in YA can hardly spell
their own names.

But amazingly enough,
things managed to work out.
More or less. I mean, for
the first time since the
accident, I actually feel
sort of optimistic. The
whole time I was in YA, I
kept imagining what it would
be like to come back to
the island and start a

relationship with Zoey. And now she's my girlfriend. It's so strange. I was there taking the rap for Claire, but Zoey was the one who was in my thoughts. I guess when you do something stupid out of love, that love fades pretty fast.

In fact, now that I think of it, most of my wishes came true. I was able to come clean about my role in Wade's death. I was able to stay on Chatham Island and graduate on time. I'm going to college. Most important, I was able to win the love of Zoey Passmore.

Of course, maintaining that love hasn't been the easiest thing in the world. Recently there have been a lot more downs than ups. Like that whole stupid thing with her diary. We

cleared it up, though—
After Zoey made me look
like a fool for believing a
false entry she put in to
set me up. I can't
believe I actually fell
for that crap about a guy
named "Antonio." Either
Zoey's a lot smarter than
I thought, or I'm a lot
more warped when I get
jealous than I thought.
Both are probably true.

Still, I was able to
convince her of the truth.
that I was looking through
her diary out of love, not
suspicion. At least I _think_
that's true. Maybe it was
one part suspicion, five
parts love. Anyway, I have
a right to be a little
suspicious every now and
then, considering what happened with Aaron Mendel.

But the true test of
my suspicion is going to come
this fall. Zoey is going to

be three thousand miles away. I'll be stuck at the University of Maine with all the losers from Weymouth High's graduating class, and she'll be on some beach in California, meeting all sorts of brilliant guys who look like <u>GQ</u> models.

Sounds like the perfect long-distance relationship, doesn't it? Maybe I'm not as optimistic as I thought.

Two

"Why isn't Jake picking up the phone?" Kate Levin demanded, to no one in particular.

Lucas stood in the front hall, staring at her as she sat on the living-room couch and twirled her long red curls absently. Suddenly she slammed the phone down on the hook. The sound of it made him jump. He frowned. For the first time since Kate had arrived from New York City to stay with the Cabrals, she was actually starting to get on his nerves.

"Look, I'm sure he's just sleeping or something," Lucas said. "Maybe the McRoyans went to the mainland today."

Kate folded her arms across her chest and grimaced. "Why wouldn't he leave me a message here? I must have left him like twenty messages last night."

Lucas shrugged. "Maybe he didn't—"

The ringing of the phone interrupted him, and Kate immediately snatched it up. "Hello?" she asked breathlessly.

Lucas watched her expression shift from eagerness to sourness in about a split second. She held the phone out at arm's length. "Lucas?" she said. "Phone. It's Aisha."

"Tell her that I still haven't heard from Christopher." Lucas shook his head. "This place is worse than an insane asylum," he muttered to himself. Aisha had been looking for Christopher all morning and somehow had it fixed in her head that he would come over to Lucas's. At least his parents weren't around. His dad was at work, and his mom was shopping in Weymouth. Well, actually it might have been a good thing if his dad *were* around because then nobody would have been yelling. Nobody would have been calling obsessively. Nobody would have even been talking. Mr. Cabral was good at two things: lobster fishing and maintaining silence in his home.

"Aisha—I *told* you, he hasn't been here," Kate was saying into the phone. "Now, if I . . ."

Without thinking, Lucas walked through the kitchen and out onto the deck that overlooked Zoey's house. He closed the sliding door behind him, shutting out the noise of Kate's yammering. The sun was directly overhead. He stretched, enjoying the cool breeze that whipped his ratty T-shirt and jeans.

Summer's almost here, he thought. And that was a good thing, too. Hopefully the weather would be nice enough for him to be outside a lot. He would need to escape this house as much as possible.

Lucas leaned over the railing and looked down at the Passmores' kitchen in hopes of catching a glimpse of Zoey. There she was—sitting at the breakfast table, hunched over a newspaper and sipping a glass of orange juice. A smile spread across his lips. Even when she was just wearing sweatpants and a T-shirt, she was stunning. He would be content to just stand here like this all day.

Zoey looked up, then saw him and smiled. She waved energetically. He waved back.

Ah, yes, he thought. *You're mine again.* He had to admit, he'd done a pretty good job last night. Not only had he managed to salvage the evening by apologizing profusely, but he'd even managed to control himself on the whole sex issue. And it hadn't been easy. After all, if any night would have been ripe to take their relationship to the next level, it was prom night. . . .

The sliding door opened behind him. Kate walked up and stood next to him as he watched Zoey disappear into the house.

"Lucas—are you throwing obscene notes at the Passmores' again?" she asked dryly.

Lucas felt himself smile. "Something like that." He should have known he wouldn't be able to stay angry at Kate for more than thirty seconds.

"What a gorgeous day," she said after a moment.

Lucas nodded. His eyes wandered out to Chatham Island's little dock area and the bluish gray ocean beyond.

"Lucas, I'm sorry if I was pissing you off this morning," she said. Her voice was quiet. "It's just that I'm upset."

"It's okay," Lucas said. Suddenly guilt washed over him for having been annoyed in the first place. After all, Kate's night had been terrible. She'd gotten a flat tire on the way to the ferry, then spent the next four hours dealing with putting on a new tire and getting the car back to the Cabrals'. By the time she'd finished, it had been far too late to go to the prom.

To make matters worse, Jake had decided to ignore her calls. But that wasn't a huge surprise. Jake McRoyan didn't need much of an excuse to get angry and act like a stubborn butthead.

"Hey, Lucas, can I tell you something?" Kate said in a voice that was barely a whisper.

Lucas swallowed. He hated questions like that. Questions like that always meant trouble. "Uh . . . what is it?"

"You have to swear to me you won't tell anyone," she said, glancing over her shoulder at the door. "I mean it."

Lucas didn't say anything. A mild queasiness was stirring in his gut. *Well, Cabral, here you go again,* he said to himself. *Time to hear another terrible secret that will put you in a really awkward position and ruin your life for a while.* He felt like laughing—or screaming.

"I didn't just get a flat tire last night," she said.

Lucas's eyes narrowed. "What do you mean?"

"Somebody ran me off the road."

Lucas blinked. He couldn't quite process what he had just heard. *"What?"*

"It was Lara," she said briskly. "I was on my way to the ferry, and suddenly I felt the car being bumped from behind. When I looked in the rearview mirror, I saw who it was."

"Are you *sure?*" Lucas asked, incredulous.

Kate nodded. "Definitely," she stated in a flat voice. "She ran me into a ditch—then sped off. But I know it was her." Kate swept her hair off her forehead, uncovering a deep purple bruise by the hairline. "I hit my head on the steering wheel when I slammed on the brakes. Pretty, huh?"

For a moment Lucas just shook his head. He was

too stunned to form any words. He'd known Lara was crazy; after all, he'd seen her at her worst—that night at Jake's when she'd been screaming drunkenly about burning Chatham Island to the ground. But he never thought she would actually try to *hurt* somebody.

"Thank God you're okay," he finally managed.

"I know." Kate took a deep breath. "I don't think she was really trying to seriously injure me or anything. I think she was just trying to scare me."

"Why would she . . ." Lucas's voice trailed off. *Jake.* Of course. Lara was completely obsessed with Jake. And her obsession—combined with general insanity and probably a quart of tequila . . . well, the scenario was beginning to make sense. He couldn't believe it. It was more than crazy; it was *sick.* "We should call the police," he said. "Lara shouldn't be allowed to get away with—"

"No," Kate interrupted firmly. "I'm serious, Lucas. I don't want anyone to know about this."

"But Kate, I—"

"Lucas, listen to me." Kate put her hand on his shoulder. "Girls like Lara . . . all they really want is attention. So if I made a big deal about this, I'd be giving her exactly what she wants. *She* wants to be seen as the victim here." She shook her head. "Believe me, I know. I've had experience with this kind of thing before."

Lucas just looked at her. None of what Kate was saying made any sense. Weren't there easier ways to get attention? If Lara wanted to look victimized, why would she *attack* somebody?

Kate squeezed his shoulder tightly. "Please, Lucas—I'm fine," she pleaded. "Just let me handle this my own way."

"Well, what if she tries something else?" he asked.

"She won't." Kate shook her head. "Trust me, she's probably a lot more freaked out than I am right now."

If she even remembers running you off the road in the first place, Lucas thought grimly. He had no doubt that Lara had been plowed at the time. There was no telling what she would do when she drank again.

Kate put her other hand on his other shoulder and shook him gently. "Don't tell anyone, okay?"

Lucas sighed. "Okay," he forced himself to say. He shook his head, staring down at her cute little porcelain face and wide blue eyes. Why was it that girls could just *look* at you, and you would automatically do anything they wanted?

"Hey—at least the car's all right," she said with a grin.

He pulled her close and gave her a hug. "Yeah, Kate," he muttered sarcastically. "I would have been really, really pissed if the car was messed up."

Kate laughed. "And if anyone asks you why I look like I've been in a street fight, just say you don't know," she insisted.

Lucas's head dropped. *Lies and secrets,* he said to himself. No matter how many times he prayed things would change, his life always ended up revolving around lies and secrets.

For only the second time since he had joined Alcoholics Anonymous, Jake McRoyan was the very first one to arrive at Sunday's meeting. The empty classroom was dark—the blinds were still drawn—and the air inside was stale and stuffy. It was hard enough coming to Weymouth High on a beautiful Sunday, but to find the room like this was especially depressing. He should have been outside—running, playing baseball, doing anything but sitting *here*. But he knew that wasn't an option.

Sighing, he raised the blinds and opened the windows, then took a seat on one of the folding metal chairs that were arranged in a neat circle in the middle of the floor.

Not since December had he felt as tempted to drink as he had the night before. When Kate had stood him up, he'd spent the rest of the night wandering aimlessly around Weymouth, lingering in front of some of his old drinking haunts. He kept thinking how it would have been so easy to buy a six-pack of beer. . . .

But he'd resisted the temptation. He supposed it was partly due to the fact that he'd spent some time sitting in the exact same spot where he'd imagined he'd seen Wade those many months ago.

Jake shivered involuntarily. He still didn't know if he'd been hallucinating or if his dead brother really *had* spoken to him from beyond the grave. But in a way, it really didn't matter. He'd gotten the message. It was either keep drinking or keep living.

The door suddenly opened. Louise Kronenberger strolled in, wearing a baggy dark blue sweat suit. Her long, curly blond hair was pulled up in a bun.

"Hey, Jake," she called cheerfully. "I was hoping you'd be early." She flopped down in the chair beside him and gave him a big smile. "Whew," she said. "I'm exhausted."

Jake just grunted. He knew he shouldn't take out his misery on Louise, but he just couldn't help it. He was in no mood for small talk.

"Hey, what's up?" she asked. She put her hand on his knee. "You all right?"

He laughed harshly. "Let's just say that my senior prom turned out a little differently than expected."

Louise swallowed. "Uh-oh," she said, withdrawing her hand. "What happened?"

"I was stood up. So I didn't go."

She peered at him closely. "Jake, you didn't—"

"No, no," he interrupted. "But believe me, I *thought* about it. A lot."

"Oh, man." She drew in her breath. "You should have come found me at the prom. We could have talked."

Jake turned to her and smiled sadly. Only Louise would think of taking time out of her own prom to comfort someone. How did she always manage to be so totally unselfish? After all, she still had to cope with the reputation of being exactly the opposite: a slut, a manipulator, and a drug fiend. Maybe she was making up for all that lost time. But then again, when she *had* been drinking and doing drugs, she must have possessed those good qualities, too. They had just been suppressed.

"I don't know how thrilled your date would have been if I had showed up and cried on your shoulder," Jake finally said.

Louise grinned. It was that wistful, regretful grin she always got whenever she thought of the past. "Yeah, I guess the entire school knows about . . . you know, what happened last fall."

Jake blushed suddenly. He hadn't been thinking about *that* at all—the time he'd lost his virginity to Louise at a party in a haze of cocaine and beer. He was just thinking that Louise's date might have been mad if some other guy had stepped in and occupied Louise's time.

"You all right?" she asked.

"Uh, yeah," he stammered awkwardly, staring at the floor. "So anyway, um—how *was* your date?"

"Well . . ."

Jake cast a sidelong glance at her. "That good, huh?"

She smiled sympathetically. "I don't want to gloat or anything."

"That's all right. Maybe it'll do me some good to hear what a normal senior prom was like. You know, from somebody who experienced it firsthand."

Louise laughed. "You know what, Jake? Let me tell you something. There are only two possible explanations for why you got stood up."

"Yeah? What?"

"Well, number one: The girl was involved in some accident or family emergency or something. Number two: She's totally insane and not worth your time in the first place. Because no girl in her right mind would leave a guy like *you* behind." She leaned over and pecked him on the cheek. "You're quite a catch, you know. I can think of about a hundred girls who would have *died* to have Jake McRoyan as their prom date."

Jake felt himself blushing again. His face was bright red. He opened his mouth, but he had no idea what to say.

"Uh-oh," Louise teased. "I embarrassed you, didn't I?"

"No, no." Jake struggled to wipe the idiotic smile off his face. "Maybe you're right—I mean, she *did* leave all these messages on my machine saying she got a flat tire."

Louise held up her hands. "See?"

"But come on, Louise. Even *I'm* not stupid enough to fall for the 'flat tire' line."

"Jake, people do get flat tires, you know. It's not like UFO abduction or anything."

"I don't know." Jake leaned forward and ran his hands through his short, wiry brown hair. "It was just . . . too convenient. You know what I mean?"

"Not really," Louise said. "Ten to one that girl is sitting at home frantically trying to get in touch with you right now."

"Maybe," Jake grumbled. But he doubted it. He knew what had happened: Kate Levin had imagined Jake McRoyan to be some kind of Prince Charming; then, when she had gotten to know him—well, naturally she had been disappointed. So then what had happened? *Boom,* flat tire. Problem solved.

"Well," Louise said. "If it's any consolation, I'll be lonely soon, too. The guy I fell in love with last night leaves for California at the end of the summer. He got a scholarship for English at UC Berkeley." She laughed once. "You know, I never imagined myself going to the senior prom with a prizewinning student."

Jake nodded, feigning interest. Hearing that definitely wasn't a consolation. It just reminded him that *his* prom date—or ex–prom date, or whatever— would be leaving at the end of the summer, too.

Of course, he probably wouldn't be seeing too much of Kate Levin in the next few months, anyway. So what did it matter?

I have to admit that I'm not all that thrilled about graduation.

I know that I should be. I mean, I'll be graduating with honors. It's pretty amazing, considering how much I slacked off this term. And I'm going to the college of my choice: Columbia. It's Ivy League, no less. And it's in New York City. For a music lover there's no place better; I'll be able to go to any concert I want. I should be ecstatic. The whole world awaits me. There's no limit to what I can do or accomplish.

Oh, I forgot. There's a slight problem. I'm blind.

When I graduate, I'll be leaving behind all these places that I've memorized—all these places I can navigate as well as any sighted person. You see, that's what makes Benjamin Passmore the Blind Wonder. You wouldn't know I was blind until you get me out of my house, or my hometown, or my school. You wouldn't know how pathetic and helpless I am until you stick me in the middle of someplace very strange and very dangerous . . . say, New York City, for example.

Do I sound bitter? Maybe I am.

But it's not only because I'm disabled or that I'm leaving familiar territory. No—leaving familiar territory shouldn't have been a problem, because my sight should have been restored. I was supposed to get my vision back. But instead I just ended up with a lot of false hopes, some very painful surgery, and lost time.

And darkness.

There's one last reason I'm bitter as well. In my anger and depression after the operation, I stupidly destroyed my relationship with Nina. I lost the one person I love more than anyone or anything in the world. And I didn't realize until very recently that if she were here with me right now, I would be able to handle anything.

I still love her—maybe even more than I ever did.

But you always want what you can't have, right? I guess I know that better than anyone.

Three

"I'm sorry, kid; I just can't help you," the hotel concierge was saying. "We don't give out the names of our guests. That's our policy."

It took all of Benjamin's effort to control himself. What was the problem with these Portsmouth hotels? He must have been to at least a dozen in the past twenty-four hours—and none of them would tell him if they had a Nina Geiger registered. Didn't they understand that a girl's life was at stake?

"I know your *policy*," Benjamin said through tightly clenched teeth. "But this girl is a runaway. People are worried about her. If she doesn't—"

"I can't help you," the man interrupted firmly. "And that's that. Now, if there's nothing else I can do for you . . ."

"What's the matter with you?" Benjamin barked, trembling. "Don't you get it?"

"Sure, I get it. Now *you* get something. If you don't leave these premises, I'm calling the cops."

Benjamin shook his head in disgust. "Don't bother," he muttered. "I'm on my way."

He swiveled around and began to tap his way toward the door with his long, thin cane. Maybe he should just give up. The whole notion of chasing after her *was* pretty hopeless, he realized. It was more than hopeless, actually; it was absurd. He almost laughed. It was truly a case of "the blind leading the blind." More like the "crazy leading the blind." Maybe he should just go home.

Once he was outside, he turned to the left and began tapping his way down the street in the direction of the bus station. A fairly strong breeze was blowing, carrying with it the faint smells of fried meat and exotic spices. Benjamin's stomach growled. He would get something to eat—then he would get on the bus back to Weymouth.

He followed the scent for another two blocks. Suddenly it grew stronger. He heard the rattling of plates, then hesitated.

"Excuse me, can I help you?" a gravelly voice beside him asked.

"Uh, yeah," Benjamin replied. "I wouldn't happen to be standing in front of a restaurant, would I?"

"You got it," the man said. "You hungry?"

Benjamin sniffed. "I was wondering what kind of smell that was. . . ."

"That's Greek. This is Niko's. It's the very best. And as you probably guessed from the way I'm talking it up, I'm Niko."

Benjamin allowed himself a grin. "Well, Niko, I'm Benjamin. And you've sold me."

"Good. Here—let me find you a seat."

Benjamin felt a hand on his arm, which guided him to a plastic chair about four feet to his immediate left. The table must have had an umbrella because Benjamin could no longer sense the sun on his skin.

"I'm just gonna put these dishes away, then I'll

come and tell you what we got," Niko said. "Back in a flash."

"Take your time," Benjamin replied. He slouched into his chair. *Finally—somebody who doesn't treat me like a five-year-old or act like a total jerk.* He felt very relieved. Why was it that so few people could deal with blindness?

It was only in the past few days that he'd truly realized how lame the majority of people on the planet were. He'd been so sheltered his entire life that he'd forgotten that most of the population never had to interact with a blind person—ever. People on Chatham Island dealt with him every day, so they had gotten used to it. It was the same with people at Weymouth High. But when he encountered strangers, his condition always provoked a reaction: pity, anger, impatience, fear . . .

What would it be like in New York?

He slipped his fingers underneath his new Ray-Ban sunglasses—the ones Nina had given him— and rubbed his eyes. He couldn't worry about college now. He had to focus on *her.*

"Hey, kid, are you all right?"

Benjamin hadn't even noticed that Niko had returned. He quickly straightened and cleared his throat. "Yeah, yeah, I'm fine," he said. "Just a little tired."

"Tired? Don't you young people sleep? You're all so *tired* all the time."

Benjamin frowned.

"Sorry, kid, no offense," Niko said with a chuckle. "It's just . . . uh, you reminded me of something, this girl who was in here this morning. She looked like she hadn't slept in about a week. A cute little thing, too—about your age. But boy, she really looked *wiped out*." He took a deep breath. "Anyway, here's what we got. I can make you a gyro with . . ."

But Benjamin wasn't listening. His pulse had quickened. *A girl my age who looked really tired. Cute. Little.* Could he be talking about Nina? It was highly unlikely . . . no, it was impossible. But still, she would fit that description, wouldn't she? And this would definitely be the kind of place where Nina would come to eat—cheap and friendly and, well, not all that healthy. *And* it was near a lot of small inns and hotels.

"Sorry," Benjamin blurted, cutting Niko off. "Did you happen to get that girl's name?"

"Yeah. Nina."

Benjamin's mouth fell open. He couldn't speak. His stomach had squeezed into a tight, painful knot.

"Why?" Niko asked, suddenly sounding concerned. "You know her?"

Benjamin nodded. "I—I'm her boyfriend," he gasped.

"Oh, boy. . . ." Niko sighed and sat down at the table. "She's a runaway, isn't she?" he asked gravely.

"How'd you know?"

"Just a hunch. She was in here a lot the past few days, at odd hours. And she loved to talk—but never about herself."

Before Benjamin knew it, he was quivering with sobs. That was Nina all right; she never wanted to talk about herself unless it was absolutely necessary. She just wanted to make jokes and talk about anything that popped into her head, to laugh . . .

"Take it easy, kid," Niko soothed. "She's okay.

36

Things are gonna work out." He put a napkin into Benjamin's hand.

Benjamin sniffed loudly and wiped his face, then let out a deep, shaky sigh. He had to gain control of himself. If this man had seen Nina, then maybe he knew where she was.

"Do you know where—"

"Boston," Niko answered before Benjamin could finish. "She left about an hour ago. She didn't say anything more specific. I'll tell you what. Why don't I fix you something to go, and then I'll take you to the bus station."

Benjamin was afraid to reply for fear he would start crying again. He bit his lip. "You don't have to do that," he finally choked. "I'll be fine."

"I'm sure you will. I'm just looking for an excuse to close up for a few minutes."

In spite of his tears, Benjamin managed a tired smile. "Okay. I guess I'm in no condition to argue."

"Good," Niko said, standing. His footsteps quickly faded away. "I'll get my car," he called.

Benjamin wiped his eyes. *Boston,* he said to himself. Why would she go there? Then again, why would she go to Portsmouth? She was just wandering thoughtlessly from one random place to the next.

Or maybe not.

Boston wasn't exactly random. It had special significance. For *both* of them. After all, they had run away there together, when Benjamin had still been keeping the whole operation at Boston General a secret. And it was on that occasion that they had slept together for the first time. . . .

"Ah!"

Without warning, a searing pain shot through Benjamin's forehead.

He let out a whimper and gripped his glasses, but suddenly it was gone. He held his breath. For the briefest instant he perceived a brilliant flash of white light.

And then it vanished.

Claire

How do I feel about graduation? I'm excited, I guess. I'll be moving on, meeting new people, and finally devoting myself to what I really want to study: meteorology and climatology.

Unfortunately I'm a little too preoccupied right now to savor the experience.

It looks as if my most ambitious plan succeeded. And I don't mean getting into MIT, or graduating with a 3.9 average, or accomplishing anything that is relatively trivial in the long run. I mean causing the breakup of my father and Sarah Mendel.

I've never felt more ashamed.

Looking back now, I can't even remember what motivated me to write that letter in the first place. I mean, I know it had to do with the anger I was feeling toward Aaron. But I've never done anything so bad and hurtful in my whole life. The thought of it literally makes me ill.

One thing is certain: I must really be in love with Aaron. That's the only possible explanation I have for acting so stupid. If I hadn't been so infatuated with him, I wouldn't have been so upset in the first place. I wouldn't have been so irrational.

Hopefully this little disaster will help me, though. I'm just now starting to realize how much I've relied on manipulating people to get what I want. I mean, I've always known it, but I've just never really allowed myself to think too deeply about it. Chatham Island is such a small place. You get to know people inside and out; you come to know their strengths and weaknesses as well as you know your own. I've always capitalized on that. I've always used it as an excuse to ensure my own happiness.

But that kind of happiness is short-lived and empty. I see that now. Maybe that's why Nina and Zoey are such happy people in general, even when they're depressed. They don't make a con-

41

cepted effort to ruin other people's
lives.

It's funny, in a way. I know
that most people think of me as the
mature Geiger sister. But Nina is
mature in ways that I'm just starting to notice. Sure, she's psychotic
and paranoid and completely insane,
but she's also sensitive and empa-
thetic. She genuinely cares for other
people. She's not afraid to show it,
either. Maybe I can even learn
from her.

Well . . .

That may be pushing it a little bit.

Four

Claire Geiger stood on the high perch of her widow's walk, staring at the ferry that was just pulling into Chatham Island from Weymouth. She chewed a nail anxiously. Usually the widow's walk was the one place in the world where she could truly relax. Here she could spend hours examining the shifting weather patterns—or just enjoy some quiet time alone. But today was not one of those days.

Aaron Mendel was on that ferry. He was coming to say good-bye to her before returning to boarding school. And if he and Claire didn't come up with a foolproof plan to reunite Burke Geiger and Sarah Mendel *fast,* she knew she could very well never see him again.

She shook her head angrily. Until very recently, the whole *point* of breaking up her father and Aaron's mother was so that she and Aaron would never have to see each other again. But as of last night Claire realized that she needed Aaron more than she had ever imagined. Sweet warmth washed over her as she remembered the way they'd held each other in that empty room of the Ambassador Hotel. . . .

But the sensation abruptly faded when she

43

remembered how the evening had ended. Claire had returned home last night at three-thirty only to find her father sitting alone in his study, crying helplessly. Apparently *he* needed *Mrs. Mendel* more than Claire had ever imagined as well.

Claire leaned over the railing and peered closely at the people getting off the ferry. Aaron was walking down the dock, talking to somebody—someone much shorter. . . .

Suddenly her heart galloped loudly in her chest.

It was his mother.

Oh, no. Claire ran a shaky hand through her long black hair. What was *she* doing with him? Hadn't she left Chatham Island for good? This was unacceptable. Claire needed to talk to Aaron—alone. They needed to pool their manipulative talents. They needed to discuss things that neither Sarah Mendel nor Burke Geiger could hear. That was why Aaron had arranged to come *now*, when Claire's father was out on the other side of the island.

Why did Aaron bring his mother with him?

Well, there was no point in obsessing about it. She just had to deal with the situation. She began pacing in little circles, then cast another quick glance at the ferry landing. Mrs. Mendel and Aaron were already on Lighthouse Road, making their way toward the house.

They would be here in a matter of minutes. At most.

I've got to think, Claire thought desperately. *Somehow I've got to divert Mrs. Mendel long enough to talk to Aaron one-on-one.*

Claire quickly bolted down the ladder and into

44

her room. How had she even gotten herself into this mess? None of this even would have *happened* if she hadn't written that stupid letter. . . .

All at once she froze.

The letter.

Of course. The letter was the key. If Claire could prove it was a fake, then Mrs. Mendel would know that Burke Geiger was an honest, faithful, and monogamous man. But how could she do it without incriminating herself?

Instinctively she dashed down the two flights of stairs to her father's study on the first floor. One by one she yanked open the drawers of the big oak desk and shuffled through the papers inside.

Damn, she thought. There was no sign of it.

In a final fit of panic and frustration she stuck her head under the desk and rooted through the wicker wastebasket. There! Her fingers closed around the familiar-looking, albeit crumpled piece of pink stationery. Her fingers trembled as she unfolded it. Yes, this was the letter; she saw "Madeline's" signature at the bottom.

A strange, unpleasant feeling gripped her body. Her eyes flashed over the page. How could she have even *thought* of doing this? She felt ashamed, repulsed. It was so cruel to her father. And in the end she had not only inflicted pain on everyone around her, but she had hurt herself as well.

The doorbell rang.

Summoning her composure, Claire shoved the paper into her jeans pocket and headed into the foyer. She cast a quick glance in the adjacent powder-room mirror to make sure her black eyes were unreadable. Then she marched over and opened the door.

45

"Hello, Claire," Mrs. Mendel said coldly.

Even in her agitated state, Claire couldn't help but notice the stark difference between Aaron and his mother. Aaron looked like a model, of course, with his solid jawline and wavy brown hair and dazzling hazel eyes. Sarah, on the other hand, looked like . . . well, a dwarf. She must have been a foot shorter than her son. All they had in common were their grim expressions.

"Hi, Mrs. Mendel," Claire said. "Hi, Aaron."

Mrs. Mendel gave her an empty smile. "Nice to see you." Her tone was stiff and formal. It was the first time she'd ever been anything but chirpy and annoying with Claire—and it made Claire nervous. "I'm just here to pick up a few things I forgot."

Aaron remained silent.

"Um . . . of course," Claire said uncertainly. "Come in." She stood aside.

"Well, dear, I'm glad I have this chance to say good-bye," Mrs. Mendel stated as she walked in.

Claire found herself at a total loss for words. She looked at Aaron—but his face was impassive.

"I'm not sure how much you overheard or what your father has told you," Mrs. Mendel continued, "but I just wanted you to know that it doesn't change my opinion of you in the least. It's been my pleasure getting to know you these past few months."

"Mrs. Mendel—can I ask you a question?" Claire found herself saying.

For a split second Mrs. Mendel's face soured.

"It's just that, uh—I mean I know it's none of my business," Claire stammered hastily. "But does any of this have to do with this letter?" She jammed her hand into her pocket and removed the piece of paper, shoving it in Mrs. Mendel's direction.

46

Mrs. Mendel's eyes were instantly ablaze. "Claire!" she barked. "What on earth—"

"I know who wrote it," Claire interrupted.

Silence enveloped the room.

Claire knew she had to make a decision *now:* either take responsibility for the letter or come up with a convincing lie. . . .

"I did it," Claire said.

Mrs. Mendel's jaw dropped.

"It was a joke—I mean, you were never supposed to see it," Claire went on. "*Nobody* was ever supposed to see it. You see, it was all part of this stupid game of Truth or Dare we were playing in Miami over spring break. Nina dared me to send a fake love letter to Dad—"

"You mean this whole thing was *your* doing?" Mrs. Mendel shrieked.

Claire felt the color draining from her cheeks. "It was just a game," she muttered, hanging her head. "We were just fooling around. I totally forgot about it the next day. I even forgot the name I used." The lie seemed to pour out of her mouth in an unnatural rush. "That's why I didn't know what you guys were talking about when you kept mentioning 'Madeline.' But this morning when I was emptying the wastebaskets, I saw it. I couldn't believe it slipped my mind. And then I realized what I might have done."

Mrs. Mendel's face twisted in disgust. "Of all the irresponsible . . ."

"I am so sorry," Claire whispered, forcing herself to look Mrs. Mendel in the eye. "I never dreamed it would get so out of hand."

"You never *dreamed?*" Mrs. Mendel snapped. "You are one very thoughtless, self-centered young lady, Claire Geiger!"

Claire winced. The words struck her like a slap in the face. But she knew there was no denying them. "I am so sorry," she repeated.

Mrs. Mendel's lips pressed into a tight line. "And what about this woman I saw—this woman holding hands with your father. Did you *dare* her as well?"

Claire sneaked a quick glance at Aaron. His eyes were wide, but he still said nothing.

"Well, I don't know about that . . . but you probably saw Jordan Kestler. She's my father's client. And believe me, there's *nothing* going on between them. She's with him right now, in fact, looking at some property she owns."

"Where?" Mrs. Mendel demanded.

"Up by Big Bite Pond," Claire replied meekly.

"Well." Mrs. Mendel's eyes narrowed. "Maybe I'll just go up there and take a look. Maybe I'll just have a chat with the both of them."

Claire nodded. "I bet it would clear everything right up—"

"Don't patronize me, Claire!" Mrs. Mendel cut in. "You have some serious answering to do for yourself when I get back." She turned to Aaron. "Wait here. This shouldn't take long."

Before Claire could utter another word, Mrs. Mendel stormed out the door and slammed it behind her.

Aisha

I cannot wait to graduate.

I'm not sure why, exactly.
I think it's mostly because
graduation represents true freedom. I mean, if you have no
idea what the future has in store
for you, you're not shackled
by any preconceptions, right?

Well, that's a slight exaggeration. I do know that I'll be at
Princeton for the next four
years. I'm just ready to put
high school behind me. I mean,
I'm obviously going to miss
Zoey and Nina. Probably more
than they know. I'm even
going to miss Claire and Lucas
and Jake and Benjamin, of course.
So let me rephrase that: I'm
ready to put all the mistakes I
made in high school behind me.

Right now, the mistake I

regret most is getting involved with David Barnes.

Don't get me wrong: David is a nice guy. Very intelligent. And sexy, in a sort of understated, intellectual way. (If that makes any sense.) But David Barnes does _not_ compare to Christopher Shupe. I could never feel the same way about David as I do about Christopher. Nobody can compare to Christopher. Period.

The only problem is that I think I might have lost him.

But I won't allow myself to believe that Christopher and I were meant for each other; I'm more sure of that now than ever. Even when I refused his proposal of marriage, which was, by the way, the most romantic proposal any girl could have ever dreamed of, I still knew he was the only man for me. I just wasn't ready for that kind of commitment.

Now my life is a little more set. I know I'm going to college fairly nearby. More important, Christopher has given up the whole crazy army business. I'm ready to get back in the swing of the relationship if he is, of course.

You know what? I think I just figured out why I'm so psyched to graduate. Once I'm done with school, I'll be able to devote myself to Christopher twenty-four hours a day.

Five

Christopher wasn't at the Cabrals' house, and he wasn't at Jimmy's—the new restaurant on Exchange Street where he had just found a job waiting tables.

Aisha stood in the bright afternoon sun on the corner of Exchange and Camden Streets and frowned. Where could he be? Lucas had told her that Christopher was supposed to be at work. Of course, knowing the way males operated, Lucas had probably been covering for him.

For a moment Aisha was nervous. Christopher wouldn't be with someone else—not so soon after the prom. Or would he? It hadn't even been a full day since he'd walked out on her. Her thoughts wandered back to the previous fall. After all, he'd found that blond floozy, whoever she was, pretty fast.

Why did I bring David to my senior prom? she wondered for maybe the millionth time.

She glanced back at Jimmy's. It wasn't all that nice. In fact, it looked kind of shabby and thrown together. And the guy who worked there seemed pretty rude. He'd only grunted and shrugged when she'd asked if Christopher was around. She doubted if the place would last very long. There was only one other real restaurant in all of North Harbor—

Passmores', the one owned and run by Zoey's parents—and it was much nicer.

A thought occurred to her then. Christopher had worked at Passmores' until he'd left; moreover, he'd loved working there. Maybe he'd gone back in hopes of finding work there again.

Aisha quickly headed toward the ferry landing, then crossed the little harbor area onto Dock Street. The restaurant door was propped open. She could hear hushed conversation and the tinkling of silverware.

"Hey, Eesh," Mrs. Passmore called when Aisha walked in. "What brings you here?"

The restaurant was about half full. Mrs. Passmore was standing by the entrance with a handful of menus, dressed in a cute flowery dress with her dark blond hair hanging over her shoulders. Aisha grinned. The dress looked like the kind of thing someone might have worn at Woodstock. Zoey was so lucky. Her parents were so cool. Aisha's own parents probably didn't even know what Woodstock *was*.

"Hi, Mrs. P.," Aisha said. "I was actually looking for someone." She began scanning the tables.

Mrs. Passmore cocked an eyebrow. "Let me guess . . . Christopher?"

"Yeah," Aisha replied hopefully. "Have you seen him?"

"As a matter of fact, I have." She pointed toward the kitchen. "He's back there talking to Jeff right now."

"Thanks." Aisha stood for a minute, shifting nervously from one foot to another. She didn't know whether to feel relieved or petrified. Christopher would definitely *not* be happy to see her.

"Hey, I'm actually looking for someone, too,"

Mrs. Passmore said quietly. "You wouldn't happen to know where Lara is, would you?"

Aisha shook her head. *No—but I can probably guess. Either passed out somewhere or enjoying the first cocktail of the day.* "Sorry," she said.

Mrs. Passmore shrugged resignedly. "Oh, well. I kinda figured you wouldn't know."

"Have you tried her apartment?" Aisha asked.

"Oh, yeah," she said flatly. "Surprisingly enough, there was no answer."

Aisha managed a sympathetic smile. "Well, if you need any help, let me know." She took a deep breath, then forced herself to move in the direction of the kitchen.

"Thanks. Hey, by the way—Zoey told me about Princeton," Mrs. Passmore called after her. "Congratulations."

Aisha just nodded in response, too nervous to speak. Her mouth had become very dry. She could hear Christopher's voice clearly now, just behind the swinging door to the kitchen. He was talking to Mr. Passmore.

". . . just wasn't working out," he was saying. "And to be honest, I really don't know about this Jimmy's place. Jimmy is kind of a jerk."

She heard the sound of Mr. Passmore laughing. "Christopher, if you're trying to ask me for your old job back, you can stop right now. The job is yours. We'd love to have you, even if it's only for a little while. You can start whenever you want. To be honest, the place hasn't been the same without you."

Christopher sighed deeply. "Whew. Thank you so much, Mr. P. You made my day."

Aisha put her hand on the door. This little exchange was a good omen, she realized. If Christopher's day was already made, then he would probably be more likely to forgive her. He sounded as if he was in a good mood. After all, he was putting his old life on Chatham Island back together, right? That meant working at Passmores', moving back into his own place . . . and last but not least, starting things back up with *her.*

But the moment she opened the door and saw Christopher's face, she knew that she was wrong. Dead wrong.

"Eesh!" Christopher spat. His brow was tightly furrowed. "What the—" Suddenly he broke off, probably because he noticed that Mr. Passmore was staring at him. "What are you doing here?" he asked, lowering his voice.

Aisha licked her lips. She glanced at Mr. Passmore, whose wide blue eyes were shifting between them. "Uh, I just wanted to talk," she said.

"Here?" Christopher cried.

Aisha swallowed. Christopher had a point. The tiny little kitchen at Passmores' was probably *not* the best place for them to work out their relationship.

"Hey, Eesh," Mr. Passmore said casually, breaking the silence. He retied the band on his gray ponytail and quickly tightened the apron that was hanging loosely over his tie-dyed shirt. "I heard about Princeton. Congratulations."

"Uh . . . thanks," she said automatically. She kept her eyes pinned to Christopher. Princeton was just about the *last* thing on her mind at this moment.

Christopher shook his head with thinly masked disgust. "I can't believe you . . . ," he muttered.

Aisha shook her head. "Christopher, I—"

"Sorry, Mr. P.," he broke in. "We'll get out of

your way. Thanks again. I really, really appreciate it." He headed for the back door.

"No problem, Christopher." Mr. Passmore nervously leaned over one of the stainless steel counters and began furiously dicing onions. "Give me a call at home later, okay? I'll see ya." He flashed a quick smile at Aisha. "Bye, Eesh."

"Bye, Mr. P.," she mumbled. *Sorry to put you through that,* she added silently. She followed Christopher out the door into the little alley outside the back of the restaurant.

"There's nothing to talk about," Christopher stated once the door was shut.

Aisha looked at the ground. "Christopher, I—"

"I mean it," he interrupted harshly. "You must really take me for a fool, you know that?"

"That's so untrue—"

"I mean, I can understand the stupid little fling you had with that geek when I was in the army," he said. "You thought it was over for us. I can even understand that you agreed to go to the prom with him before you knew I was coming back. I mean, personally, I think your taste has suffered in ways that defy the imagination—but at least I can understand it."

In spite of her misery, Aisha couldn't help but feel a trace of amusement. Even when Christopher Shupe was unsure of something as important as his love life, he was still absolutely sure of one thing: himself.

"But what I can't understand—and what I can't forgive—is the lying." His voice rose. "You *lied* to me, Eesh. You *promised* you were gonna end it with that . . ." He abruptly trailed off in midsentence. "Oh, no," he mumbled.

Aisha looked up.

Christopher was staring over her shoulder toward Dock Street. She whirled around.

Lara was walking down the alley. Well, not quite walking. Stumbling was more like it.

"Oh, jeez," Aisha whispered.

"Wassup, guys?" Lara sang out, grinning crookedly. Her hair was unkempt, hanging in her eyes. She was wearing the shortest black miniskirt Aisha had ever seen.

"You're not planning on *working* today, are you, Lara?" Christopher demanded fiercely.

"As a matter of—" All of a sudden Lara lost her balance and went tumbling right into Christopher's arms. "Whoa!" she shrieked. She giggled maniacally as he propped her back on her feet.

Aisha's nose wrinkled. She took a few steps back, totally aghast. Even from where she was standing, the stench of alcohol was overpowering.

"Jesus!" Christopher barked. He gripped Lara by the shoulders. "What the hell are you thinking? You *stink!*"

Lara shook her head. With a frantic twist she wrenched herself free of his grasp. Her body went flying back against the wall, but somehow she managed to stay standing. "Thass not . . . thass not very polite," she said, gasping for breath.

"Polite?" Aisha cried. "Lara, just look at yourself. There's no way you can go in there—"

"Who assed you, bitch?" Lara slurred.

"Hey!" Christopher yelled. "Don't talk—"

"Oh, shut up." She glared unsteadily at him. "I know why you're here. You comin' to steal my job. You sneaky little . . . well, lemme tell you somethin'—the job's mine. And you can't have your apartment back, either." Her voice rose to a shout.

"So you and your little miss girlie-girl here can take a hike!"

Christopher's jaw dropped.

Aisha wanted to say something—but she couldn't. She was too shocked to do anything but watch Lara slam the kitchen door behind her. Her eyes drifted over to Christopher. Their gazes locked.

"Are you all right?" she breathed.

Christopher hesitated, then shook his head. "Maybe we should go in there. . . ."

"Or maybe we should listen to her," Aisha said quickly. "Maybe we should take a hike." She felt bad for the Passmores, but Lara wasn't *their* problem. She couldn't deal with a problem like that right now. Neither could Christopher. They had enough problems of their own.

Finally Christopher nodded. "Maybe you're right."

Zoey was just putting on her sandals to go to Lucas's house when the doorbell rang.

"Coming!" she yelled, running down the stairs. "Who is it?"

"Lucas," came the soft reply.

"Hey!" She threw the door open and gave him a kiss. "I was just on my way to see you. We must have a psychic connection."

Lucas gave her a halfhearted smile. "I guess so," he said, brushing his hair out of his eyes.

She frowned. "What's wrong? Are you okay?"

Lucas shrugged. He walked in and immediately stretched out on the living-room couch. "Let's just say it's been a rough morning," he said with a groan, closing his eyes. "Sometimes it's kind of hard having a roommate, y'know?"

Zoey sighed. *Poor Lucas.* She came over and sat

beside him on the armrest. "Yeah, what's going on? Weren't Kate and Jake supposed to go to the prom together?" she asked softly, running her fingers through his blond curls.

"Not the best." He grinned. "Mmmm. That feels nice."

Zoey leaned over and planted a delicate kiss on his lips. "How does that feel?" she whispered.

"I knew I had a good reason for coming over here," he said. He reached for her, wrapping his arms around her neck and drawing her close. "I just need another reminder. . . ."

The phone started ringing.

Zoey laughed. "Perfect timing," she muttered.

Lucas kept his arms around her. "Let's just let the machine pick up," he said in a husky voice. "I need to be consoled."

"I should really answer it. . . ." She gently removed his hands and headed for the kitchen. She decided not to add the reason: that she was secretly hoping the caller would be Nina or Benjamin—or best of all, both of them together.

"Hello?"

"Lara's drunk again," her father's brusque voice hissed at the other end.

"Oh, God." Zoey's stomach dropped. "What happened?"

"She staggered in here a few minutes ago and ended up vomiting all over the kitchen."

Zoey gasped. "Are you *serious?*"

"Unfortunately, yes. Your mother is taking her home right now. Christopher and Aisha were just here—but now I can't find them. So—"

"I'll be right there. I'll bring Lucas, too. Maybe he can help."

"That would be great, honey. Tell him that we'll pay him, of course."

"All right. See you in a few minutes." Zoey hung up the phone and marched back into the living room.

Lucas was already sitting up, looking worried. "What's up?" he asked.

"Lara. She's drunk." Zoey laughed dismally. "Surprise, surprise. My mom's taking her home, so I need to go to the restaurant." She paused. "Lucas, I, uh . . ."

"Volunteered my services?" he asked, raising his eyebrows. "I heard. No problem. I'm happy to help. Just as long as it doesn't involve cleaning up after Lara. I've had enough experience with *that* already."

"Um . . . right." Zoey nodded. Maybe she should have asked her father if the vomit was all cleaned up.

Lucas started laughing. "You know, I'm really glad we have this chance to enjoy a nice, romantic postprom Sunday."

Zoey just looked at him. "I wish I could laugh at that," she moaned. "But it's just too depressing."

Without another word Lucas hopped up and kissed her on the forehead, then headed out the door.

At least I have Lucas, she thought as she followed him. *Lara may have singlehandedly ruined my parents' business; my brother and my best friend may be lost forever—but at least I have Lucas.*

Zoey slipped her hand into his once they were outside. Their fingers intertwined as they headed down the cobbled stones of Camden Street onto South Street.

"You know, I just don't get it," she murmured distractedly. "Lara hasn't done this since before she moved out."

Lucas looked dubious. "Are you sure?"

"I mean, she's gotten drunk plenty of times—but she hasn't showed up for work totally wasted in months. Something must have happened. . . ."

Lucas's hand seemed to tense. He quickly looked away.

Zoey looked at him closely. His eyes had taken that shifty, frightened quality they always got when he was hiding something. She slowed down a little.

"Lucas?"

"What is it?" he asked, blinking.

"You know something, don't you," Zoey said.

"Uh . . . what do you mean?"

She let go of his hand. "Come on, Lucas. This is important."

"Well—maybe Lara's just upset because Jake and Kate are going out. Maybe she's drinking away her sorrows."

Zoey stopped walking altogether. She hadn't even thought of that—but it was probably true. It was also a pretty astute observation for Lucas, especially considering he never thought about other people's business unless it was absolutely necessary. She peered at him. He still looked as if he were holding something back. And what had happened between Jake and Kate, anyway? Zoey hadn't seen them all night. After all, Lucas would know; Kate was his housemate.

"What?" Lucas asked.

"It *does* have something to do with Jake and Kate, doesn't it?" Zoey asked.

Finally Lucas sighed. "Look," he said. "You have to swear to me you won't make a big deal out of this, all right? Kate would kill me."

Zoey nodded, feeling nervous. A series of images flashed through her mind: Kate and Jake skipping the prom altogether and hopping into the sack at Jake's house—only to have Lara burst in on them. . . .

"Lara ran Kate off the road last night," Lucas said. "She did it to keep Kate from going to the prom with Jake."

Zoey paused. "You want to run that by me again?"

"I know; it sounds crazy. But I'm telling you— that's what happened. She ran Kate into a ditch, and she got a flat tire."

She ran Kate into a ditch? Zoey was almost too stunned to respond. "Is . . . is Kate all right?"

Lucas snorted. "Yeah—considering the fact that she missed the prom and spent the whole night dealing with the car. *And* considering Jake hasn't returned a single one of her calls."

"Jeez." Zoey stared at him. "She's really sick."

He nodded. "No kidding. But for some reason, Kate doesn't want anyone to know about it." He threw his hands up in the air. "She has some crazy theory about how Lara *wants* people to find out. She thinks the whole reason Lara did it in the first place was to get attention. I mean, what's *that* all about?"

"It makes sense, Lucas." Zoey took his hand again.

"What?" Lucas shouted.

Zoey nodded. She knew exactly where Kate was coming from. Lara was clearly prepared to do any-thing—*anything*—to make Jake feel sorry for her. And to keep Jake and Kate apart.

"It's true, Lucas," she said. "Lara just wants to do something that will make everyone notice her."

"Whatever. Maybe you're right. Just swear to me you won't tell anyone, Zoey." Lucas's voice was void of humor. "I mean it."

Zoey paused. She didn't want to betray Lucas's

trust—especially after the fight they had just been through the week before—but at the same time Lara couldn't be allowed to get away with something like this. Lara McAvoy had clearly graduated from being a drunken nuisance to being a drunken lunatic.

"Okay," Zoey finally agreed. "But Lucas, you have to promise me something, too. Promise me you'll talk to Kate. Promise me you'll try your best to convince her to let people know about this."

Lucas hesitated.

"I mean it, Lucas."

He nodded gravely. "Okay. I promise."

JAKE

I'm not quite sure how I feel about graduation. I guess it doesn't seem totally real to me yet. Maybe that's because it's still so far in the future. I mean, I know it's only like a month, but if you're a recovering alcoholic, a _week_ seems like a long time.

All in all, I'm pretty happy, though. For a while there I was positive I wouldn't even live to see spring break. But thanks to A.A., not to mention a little help from my friends and family, I made it. I was even able to get an athletic scholarship at U Mass. (I think Coach McNair was as shocked as I was.)

The only thing that bothers me is that Wade won't be there to see the graduation ceremony. I think he would have gotten a big kick out of it. He was the one who was always telling me I would never amount to anything. I know he would have been proud. Of course, he probably wouldn't have told me—but I know it, anyway.

I guess there's one

other little thing that
bothers me, too.

All through high school I
always pictured myself
graduating with the girl of
my dreams.

For the first three
years, of course, I thought
that girl was going to be
Zoey. I actually thought
we were going to get <u>mar-
ried.</u> Looking back now, it
seems pretty silly. I mean,
I still love her, and I
always will. Just not in
that way.

Then there was Claire.
All I can say about Claire
is that I should have known
better. I don't think she
ever really liked me in

the first place. She was
just using me for reasons
that I still don't know and
are probably way over my
head.

And then Lara came
along. There was a time
when I really thought Lara
was the one. Even when I
was sober. Ha, ha, ha. But
seriously, I thought that
Lara and I would be able
to help each other out.
But then I realized that
Lara needs a lot more
help than I can give her.

And finally there was
Kate. I don't think I've
ever fallen for anyone
harder. She was—and still
is—the most beautiful girl

I've ever seen. Not to mention the funniest, brightest, and most sophisticated.

But you know what I realized, even before she stood me up?

Why would a girl like Kate Levin ever want to go out with a guy like Jake McRoyan?

Six

By the time Jake got home from Weymouth, he was exhausted. The meeting had lasted longer than usual. A couple of people had admitted to relapsing. The stories they told were painful and sordid, but Jake had been happy to stay and hear them. Listening to those people made him all the more relieved that he'd resisted the urge to drink himself.

He stretched out on his bed and closed his eyes. Brilliant shafts of afternoon sunlight were pouring through the sliding glass doors of his room, but he had no doubt that he'd be able to fall asleep fast. After all, he'd barely slept the night before.

I'm not going to get angry anymore, he thought, yawning. *It could have been worse. I'm not quite sure how, but it could have been worse. Kate could have showed up at the prom with another guy—*

"Jake?" his father yelled from upstairs. "Is that you?"

Jake groaned. "Yeah, Dad," he called back. "The meeting ran a little late. I'm just going to take a nap, okay?"

"Before you take a nap, you *must* call this girl

Kate," his father stated firmly. "She's been calling the house all day. She's starting to drive me crazy."

"All right, all right," Jake mumbled. He rolled over and pulled the pillow over his head.

"*Now,* Jake," Mr. McRoyan insisted.

"Okay, okay, fine." Jake tossed the pillow aside and reached for the phone by his bed. His dad was right; it would be better to get this over with. What was the big deal, anyway? She was probably just calling to tell him that she'd been thinking things over and that she'd decided that she didn't want to be "in a relationship" right now. Girls were always coming up with meaningless excuses like that.

He punched in Lucas's number. After four rings the answering machine picked up. *"You've reached the Cabral residence,"* Mr. Cabral's Portuguese-accented voice announced. *"Please leave—"*

Jake slammed the phone back down on the hook.

"She's not home, Dad," he yelled. He closed his eyes again.

Even though he hated to admit it, he was relieved. He would be much happier if he never had to talk to Kate Levin again.

Just as he was starting to drift into unconsciousness, there was a knock on the glass door. He glanced up—then jerked awake with a start.

It was *her.*

She pointed at the door handle.

"It's open," he called.

Kate pulled open the door and stepped in quickly, then shut it, averting her eyes. Jake sat up in bed.

"Uh, I'm sorry to bother you if you were sleeping or something," she said.

"It's okay." He rubbed his eyes, wishing very much that Kate didn't look so beautiful. A few strands of long, curly red hair were hanging in her face. She was wearing an extremely sexy one-piece black dress with two shoulder straps—the kind of thing girls on Chatham Island *never* wore. Suddenly he realized he was staring at her. He looked away.

"Look, Jake," she began, "I'm sorry to barge in on you like this. But I have to talk to you."

She paused, as if waiting for a response—but Jake said nothing.

"I don't know why you've been blowing off my calls," she continued. "But if you think it's because I stood you up last night, you couldn't be more wrong."

"I don't know where I got the idea you stood me up," he said sarcastically. "I mean, I must be crazy or something—"

"I got a flat tire!" she cried. "What do you want me to say? Call Lucas if you don't believe me. Call Mr. Cabral. *He'll* tell you about meeting me on Dock Street and towing the car out of the ditch and putting the new tire on."

Jake gazed at the rumpled sheets on the bed. He'd sworn to himself after all the misery he'd been through with Lara that he'd never fall for any girl's line again—no matter how convincing. "Fine," he said quietly. "I believe you. But what I don't understand is why you didn't get on the water taxi. What I don't understand is why you didn't try to call the Ambassador Hotel and page me."

"Jake—Lucas told me you didn't even *go* to the hotel," she pleaded. A teasing laugh escaped her lips. "Come on, you're being—"

"So you think it's funny?" he barked, glaring at her. "I'm glad. Yeah, it's a real comedy, Kate. I'm happy you're enjoying yourself."

Her smile faded. "That's not what I meant. I'm just saying . . ." She shook her head. "Look, I don't know what I'm saying. I just want a chance to apologize. If you only knew how much I didn't want things to turn out like this. . . . Jake, I wanted to go to that prom with you so much. I mean it."

Jake lay back down and pulled the covers over himself. He squeezed his eyes tightly shut. "I guess *so* much just wasn't quite enough."

"If you—"

"I'm tired, Kate. I need to sleep, all right? I'll call you later."

"So what does this mean?" she asked.

"It means I'm tired," he said flatly.

There were a few seconds of silence, then he heard the door slide open. "I'm sorry." Kate's voice was barely a whisper. "I was really hoping things were going to work out between us."

Jake opened his mouth to say something else, but the door had already slid shut.

Benjamin was in a complete and utter daze. He was vaguely aware from the way the bus was slowing down and turning that it must be nearing Boston—but he'd hardly noticed the passage of time. His mind was whirling one moment and totally blank the next. He'd even managed to forget about Nina. Not much, but a little.

What had the flash of light meant?

It wasn't totally unprecedented, he realized. He'd experienced something nearly identical—without the pain, of course—when Dr. Martin had removed his bandages on that fateful day in January.

His most recent flash was different in another way, too.

In that brief instant he'd thought he'd seen something besides a haze of formless light. It had happened so fast, but in that tiny space of time he'd thought he'd seen the faint outline of something flat and circular.

He thought he'd *seen* something.

Benjamin licked his dry lip, struggling to breathe evenly. Could it have been his imagination? It very well might have been. But he had been sitting at a circular table; he'd known that from touching it. Had he seen it? Had he really, truly seen it?

He shook his head and ran his sweaty palms on his pants leg. When Niko had dropped him off at the bus station, Benjamin could barely talk. The guy had probably thought it was because Benjamin was so stricken with grief. That was partially true, obviously—but now Benjamin was not only scared for Nina, he was terrified for himself.

There's no reason to be scared. It's not as if my condition can get any worse. I can't get more blind.

But the pain had been scary—mostly because it had been so totally unexpected. Would there be more of it?

The bus slowed to a crawl, and Benjamin sensed from a shift in his weight that it was making a sharp turn. He heard the faint screech of tires. "Boston, Massachusetts," the bus driver announced over the loudspeaker. "Now arriving in Boston."

There was another turn, and then the bus jerked to a halt. Benjamin heard a soft, steamy hiss as the engine died.

Maybe it was a lucky twist of fate that Nina had decided to drift to Boston, he realized. He stood and began making his way carefully down the narrow aisle toward the door. If something were seriously wrong with him, he could just go see Dr. Martin. In fact, he could call Dr. Martin right now. He still remembered Boston well enough to get to two places: the Malibu Hotel and Boston General Hospital. Those were all he needed.

After easing himself down the steep steps of the bus he pulled out his cane and tapped it in front of him, following the sounds of other people's footsteps.

"Do you need any help, son?" an elderly woman's voice asked beside him.

"Actually, yes, thank you," Benjamin said gratefully. "Can you tell me where a telephone is, please?"

"Certainly." The woman put a hand on his arm and steered him through a door, then paused a few paces later. "Here you are."

"Thanks," Benjamin said. He hesitated for a moment. He wanted to call his family and let them know he was all right—but was that really true? He certainly didn't feel "all right." He felt sweaty and shaky and anxious. But if he told his parents and Zoey about the mysterious flash, wouldn't they just panic? They would probably insist on doing something crazy—like coming down here to get him. On the other hand, they had a right to know. He had just taken off without even really getting permission first. They would never be able to forgive themselves if something happened to him.

Finally he reached over and picked up the phone. He punched in his family's credit card number and waited. After the fourth ring the answering machine picked up. *"Hello, there! You've reached the Passmores. . . ."*

Benjamin sighed. *Thank God for answering*

machines, he thought. There was nothing like a one-way conversation to avoid potentially sticky situations. The machine beeped. He took a deep breath.

"Uh, hi, everyone," he said uncertainly. "I just got into Boston. . . . Luckily I ran into this guy who had seen Nina, and he told me she was headed here. . . ." He chewed the inside of his mouth. "So, uh, I'll call you later to let you know if I find out anything. I'll be staying at the Malibu Hotel." He dropped the phone back on the hook.

He frowned. Why had he chickened out? He was half tempted to pick up the phone and call back. But no . . . he would talk to Dr. Martin and *then* call, so he would have something concrete to tell them. Speculation wouldn't do anybody any good.

But first he needed to check into the Malibu Hotel.

He stood in front of the phone for a moment, seemingly unable to move. An odd mix of sadness and apprehension had seized him. *The Malibu Hotel.* He knew the smell and feel of that place were going to recall some powerful memories.

And worst of all, he would have to deal with them alone.

Nina wasn't sure why she had chosen room 428. She wasn't even sure why she had chosen the Malibu Hotel. As a matter of fact, she had no idea why she had come to Boston in the first place. The notion had just popped into her head while she'd been talking to Niko—and now she was here.

It was nearly five o'clock. The sun had already begun to sink in the sky, casting long shadows across the dusty room. At least the Malibu Hotel was an improvement over that dump where she had stayed in Portsmouth. Not much of an improvement, of course, but enough.

Nina pulled a Lucky Strike out of her pocket and stuck it in her mouth, then lay down on the huge queen-size double bed. The mattress cover was still the same puke yellow she remembered from her last visit. She stared at the ceiling and sucked on the cigarette absently. This bed was pretty big for one person. Too big, actually. She could get lost in this stupid bed.

"What am I doing here?" she asked out loud. The words echoed hollowly against the bare walls.

It's Sunday. I have school tomorrow, for God's sake. Who knows—I could be missing an algebra exam. I could be missing an important school function, like voting for which cheerleader has the best breast implants.

She laughed once. Even if she were to jump out of this bed right now, rush back to the bus station, and catch the next bus to Weymouth, she wouldn't get there until after midnight. The last ferry left Weymouth at nine. That meant she would have to take the water taxi to get back to Chatham Island—and that would cost her forty dollars. She only had thirty-eight and some change in cash.

Nope—it was out of the question. Even if she wanted to go home tonight, she couldn't.

She glanced at the phone by her bed. The last time she'd called her house had been three days ago. Maybe it would be a good idea to check in again.

For some reason, she had been thinking about her father a lot in the past few hours. She remembered how worried he had been when he found out about Uncle Mark—and she hadn't even run away then. It was pretty amazing, when she thought of it. Seeing one's ex-boyfriend kiss another girl wasn't even in the same league as what Uncle Mark had done, yet Benjamin's kiss had compelled her to run away. Why had she reacted so strongly now? Was she somehow weaker?

Maybe she was. But she had always been fragile; she could admit that to herself. She knew she needed to check in with her father, if only to hear his voice. After all, for all she knew, he and the midget could have gotten married in her absence.

Nina reached over and picked up the phone, then punched zero.

"Yes?" a whiny operator's voice asked.

Nina rolled her eyes. Why was it that all phone operators sounded like members of The Chipmunks? "I'd like to make a collect call, please." She gave the operator the number.

"Whom should I say is calling?" the operator asked.

"Um . . . Hulk Hogan."

The phone rang twice, then there was a click. "Hello?" Claire answered.

"I have a collect call from a Miss Hulk Hogan," the operator said. "Do you accept the charges?"

Claire groaned. "Yes," she stated tonelessly. "Hello, Nina."

"Jeez, Claire, I'm thrilled to talk to you, too," Nina said. "Don't worry; I'm fine."

"I *know* you're fine." Claire's voice was curt. "You wouldn't be making stupid jokes if you weren't fine. Now when are you coming home?"

Nina's smile faded. She suddenly felt sick. In that moment she saw herself in stark, objective clarity: She was a spoiled brat who had gone too far. Running away was the most stupid, selfish, childish thing she had ever done. Not to mention dangerous. Her family was sick with worry, and she was making wisecracks. What was she *doing?*

"I'm sorry," she whispered. "Claire—I'm coming home tomorrow. I'd come tonight, but I'm in Boston."

"Boston? What are you doing . . ." Claire sighed. "Never mind." Her tone softened. "Are you all right?"

"Fine," she said quickly. "I've never felt better, actually. I think I've found the new miracle weight-loss program: running away, living on gyros, no sleep—"

"Nina, Sarah walked out on Dad," Claire interrupted.

Nina's eyes widened. The cigarette fell out of her mouth. *"What?"* she cried. "Why?"

"It's a long story."

Nina was instantly gripped by a horrible, sinking feeling. Could *she* have been the reason? Maybe Sarah left because the Geiger household was in such turmoil. Maybe she didn't want to deal with a totally dysfunctional stepdaughter—someone who would freak out and disappear at a moment's notice.

"It was my fault. I sort of engineered the whole thing," Claire continued quietly. "But I really don't want to get into the sordid specifics right now."

"Uh, what did you say?" She grimaced.

"I'll tell you *later,* Nina," Claire said.

Nina gazed blankly into space. It was Claire's fault? She shook her head. Claire had done something to make Sarah Mendel walk out on their father? She'd always known Claire to be devious—but this . . . this was a new level of deceit, even for her. Burke Geiger had been in love, truly happy for the first time since their mother's death. Nina cringed. Claire really *didn't* stop at anything to get what she wanted. But then again, Nina wasn't in much of a position to pass judgment on her older sister at this moment. She was no better.

"Nina?" Claire asked. "Are you there?"

"Yeah. Um . . . is Dad home right now?"

"No," Claire said nervously. "That's the thing. I told Sarah my part in it—well, *most* of it, anyway—and she stormed out of here looking for him. That was about five hours ago. I'm worried she might have done something drastic."

"Claire, Sarah isn't exactly the vengeful, gun-wielding type."

"I *know* that." She sounded exasperated. "But she does have a temper. I experienced it firsthand this morning. I'm just worried, all right?"

Nina shook her head. "This is crazy," she muttered.

"You're telling me. Look, I should go. Aaron's here, and he's about to leave."

"Okay." Nina thought for a moment. There was nothing she could do right now to ameliorate the situation. All she could do was try to get a good night's sleep and leave first thing in the morning. "Look, just tell Dad that I'm fine and I'll be home as soon as possible. If he absolutely has to get in touch with me, I'm at the Malibu Hotel. And tell Zoey and Eesh that I'll be back tomorrow, all right?"

"All right," Claire said. "I will. Bye, Nina."

"Bye. I hope everything works out."

"Me too." The line went dead.

Nina hung up the phone and stuck the cigarette back into her mouth. She couldn't believe it. She'd been away for a week, and her family had completely fallen apart.

Well, at least there was one positive element to all this.

Family crises did wonders for making one forget about lame ex-boyfriends.

Seven

"How's Nina?" Aaron asked.

Claire blinked, shaking her head. She'd been sitting in silence after hanging up the phone, staring at it, lost in thought. "She's fine," she said, returning to the harsh reality of the Geiger living room. "She's coming home tomorrow."

Aaron smiled hopefully. "Well, that's good."

"I guess." Claire shrugged. "I just hope she has something nice to come home to."

Aaron nodded. He cast a glance out the front window, then sat next to Claire on the couch. "It's getting late, Claire. I really should leave soon. I can't check into my dorm any later than ten without getting into trouble."

Claire glanced at the clock. It was already five-fifteen. Where could her father and Aaron's mother possibly be? "You just missed the five-ten ferry," she said. "The next one's at seven-forty."

Aaron drew in his breath anxiously. "I don't know if I can wait that long," he said. "I might have to take the water taxi. . . ."

Claire took his hand. "Please wait with me, Aaron," she murmured.

He hesitated for a moment. "I will. Don't worry."

He put his arm around her and gathered her close to him, then kissed her on the cheek. "You know, I've never seen my mother get mad like that. *Ever.* She must really be in love with your dad. So that's a good sign, I guess."

Claire raised her eyebrows. "You think? Yeah, I guess she's in love with him. Like Medea was in love with Jason. In love enough to kill him. She's probably burying the body out by Big Bite Pond right now. . . ."

"Claire! Come on. Look, why would she even be mad at your dad, anyway? She's mad at *you,* remember?"

Claire nodded grimly. "Oh, yes. I remember."

Aaron put his fingers under her chin and gently turned her head so that she was looking directly into his hazel eyes. "Look, Claire, no matter what happens tonight—I just want you to know . . . I think it's amazing what you did here this morning."

"Amazing?" Claire sneered. "Try stupid."

"Not at all. You took responsibility for what you did. You came clean." His expression grew thoughtful. "I don't know if I would have done the same thing."

"You wouldn't have written that letter in the first place," Claire mumbled. "You wouldn't have done something so twisted."

A little half smile curled on his lips. He let his hand drop. "Wanna bet?"

Claire found herself smiling, too. "Well, okay— maybe you would have. But it doesn't matter. Anyway, you're wrong. I didn't come clean. I still lied."

"That's true," Aaron conceded. He looked at the floor. "But that doesn't matter. You made my mother

82

realize that your dad wasn't to blame—and that we were. Or that *you* were. You didn't even bring me into it."

"You didn't write the letter."

"Yeah, but I knew about it. I could have done something. So in a way I was just as responsible."

Claire just looked at him. Was this really the same Aaron Mendel whom she had met last December—the schemer who put on a different face for every new person he met? He was, she reflected, but he had changed. He'd given up trying to lie to her. He'd given up trying to be anything but straightforward because he knew nothing else would work. They were both too clever.

"What are you thinking?" he asked.

She swallowed. "I'm thinking how much I don't want to lose you," she breathed.

He planted a soft kiss on her lips. "You won't, Claire."

She was just about to kiss him again when she heard the familiar roar of an engine. Instantly they sprang apart. Claire leaped off the couch and faced the window. She stared in numb fear as her father's Mercedes pulled to a halt in front of the house.

Her father got out of the car and slammed the door, then walked over to the passenger side.

Claire held her breath.

Then her eyes widened.

Her father was *smiling*.

Yes, he was smiling broadly as he helped Sarah Mendel out of the car. For a moment they stood next to the door, holding hands. Then Mr. Geiger took her in his arms and kissed her passionately.

Aaron grabbed Claire's arm. "Look!" he cried, bouncing up and down. "Look!"

Claire just shook her head, unable to speak. She could only gape as her father and Aaron's mom made their way up the porch steps, arm in arm. A moment later the front door opened.

"Hello?" Mr. Geiger called, walking tentatively into the foyer. "Anyone home?"

Aaron let his hand fall away from Claire's arm. "Right here," he said.

Mr. Geiger turned to Claire. His expression became somber. Their gazes locked.

For a brief instant Claire was reminded of the old Burke Geiger—the solemn, quiet man he had become after her mother's death, before he had met Sarah Mendel. Then Sarah stepped into the foyer. She closed the door and stood next to him.

A faint smile played on Mr. Geiger's lips. "Well, Claire, I must say . . . I'm really at a loss for words," he said slowly. "But we'll talk about all *that* later, when your sister comes home. I'll start with the good news." He paused. "Sarah and I have decided that it's pointless to wait any longer. We're going to get married next weekend."

"Oh, my . . ." The next thing Claire knew, she was rushing over to him, throwing her arms around his neck. "Dad, that is so great," she whispered. She squeezed her eyes tightly shut. "I am so happy for you."

Mr. Geiger patted her back gently, then stepped back and cleared his throat. "I think you owe some-one an apology," he stated.

Claire nodded. She turned and forced herself to look Sarah in the eye. "Mrs. Mendel, if there's any way I can make it up to you . . ."

Mrs. Mendel wasn't smiling, but her eyes were soft. "Well, Claire, I suppose you can. You father and I are going to need a lot of help planning this event. A big chunk of the responsibility is going to fall on you." She paused. "And I owe you an apology, too. I was out of line taking that tone with you this morning. I guess my emotions just got the better of me." She extended her hand. "Friends again?"

Claire clasped it with both hands. For the first time since she had met Mrs. Mendel, Claire wasn't privately addressing her as "the midget" or "Tattoo" or "birdbrain."

We never really became friends in the first place, she thought. But she swore to herself right then and there that she was going to do her best to get along with Sarah—for her own sake, as well as for her father's and Aaron's.

"Friends," she agreed.

Aaron appeared at his mother's side and put his arm around her shoulders. He was beaming triumphantly. "Congratulations!"

"Now, this is more like it," Sarah said. "Now we can concentrate on being a family again."

"That's right," Mr. Geiger chimed in.

Claire found that her eyes were wet. Since when had she gotten so emotional? Normally she would have been able to view a scene like this with cool detachment. After all, everything had gone according to plan. The reconciliation was just a matter of all the pieces finally falling together.

"I suppose this calls for a celebration." Mr. Geiger was smiling, but for some reason his face seemed vaguely troubled. "Although I don't feel quite right about celebrating when Nina isn't here."

"She just called," Claire said. "She's coming home tomorrow. She's fine. She's at a hotel in Boston—the Malibu Hotel."

Mr. Geiger sighed deeply. "Does she want me to call her?"

"She said only if you wanted to."

"Well." He straightened his shoulders. All at once a huge, uninhibited smile broke across his face. "I guess what started out as a pretty lousy day is turning out all right after all."

Christopher

I DIDN'T GIVE MUCH THOUGHT TO GRADUATION. I WAS JUST EXCITED TO GET THE HELL OUT OF BALTIMORE. I HARDLY EVEN REMEMBER THE CEREMONY— EXCEPT FOR THE AWARDS PART, OF COURSE. I'LL NEVER FORGET THE EXPRESSION ON SOME OF THOSE KIDS' FACES. WHO WOULD HAVE THOUGHT THAT AN AFRICAN-AMERICAN WOULD WALK OFF WITH A PRIZE IN MATHEMATICS?

BUT I GUESS THEY HAD THE LAST LAUGH, THOUGH. THEY'RE ALL GOING TO BE SOPHOMORES AT JOHNS HOPKINS OR YALE OR HARVARD. HERE I AM—ALMOST BROKE AND AN ARMY DROPOUT, WITH NO IDEA WHERE I'LL BE IN THE NEXT YEAR, LET ALONE THE NEXT MONTH. A LOT OF GOOD THOSE HONORS ARE DOING ME NOW.

WHEN I MOVED UP TO MAINE LAST SUMMER, MY PLAN WAS SIMPLE: WORK MY BUTT OFF FOR A YEAR AND SAVE TONS OF MONEY SO THAT I WOULD ONLY HAVE TO ASK FOR A PARTIAL SCHOLARSHIP WHEN I APPLIED TO COLLEGE.

IT WOULD HAVE WORKED, TOO. BUT

THERE WAS AN UNEXPECTED PROBLEM. I DIDN'T COUNT ON MEETING AISHA GRAY.

YEAH, I GUESS YOU COULD SAY THAT SHE DID AN EXTREMELY THOROUGH JOB OF RUINING MY LIFE. AFTER ALL, SHE WAS THE REASON I DECIDED TO GIVE UP WORK, BUY A RING, AND JOIN THE ARMY. AND WHY? BECAUSE I STUPIDLY THOUGHT SHE WAS ACTUALLY GOING TO MARRY ME.

AND YOU KNOW WHAT THE REALLY PATHETIC THING IS?

I CRAWLED BACK TO THIS ISLAND TO WIN HER BACK. EVEN AFTER SHE REFUSED TO BE MY WIFE, I STILL CAME BACK. ALL THIS, WHILE SHE'S RUNNING AROUND WITH SOME LAME GEEK BEHIND MY BACK.

IT'S AMAZING. IN ALL THE NINETEEN YEARS OF MY LIFE, I'VE THOUGHT OF MYSELF AS MANY THINGS: BRILLIANT, AMAZINGLY GOOD LOOKING, TALENTED. . . . WELL, OKAY, MAYBE THAT'S A SLIGHT EXAGGERATION.

BUT I NEVER THOUGHT OF MYSELF AS A CHUMP.

NOT UNTIL I SAW AISHA GRAY MAKING OUT WITH DAVID BARNES A WEEK AFTER SHE TOLD ME SHE'D LOVE ME FOREVER.

Eight

Christopher sat on the beach on the other side of Leeward Drive, staring across the water as the sun drew closer and closer to the buildings and rooftops of Weymouth. Aisha sat next to him, digging her feet absently into the sand. He was starting to get annoyed. When he'd suggested that the two of them go somewhere to talk, he hadn't thought that she'd hang around with him for the entire afternoon. Of course, the conversation hadn't really gone the way he had originally intended.

First they'd talked about the whole Lara incident, which led to a discussion about how cool the Passmores were for putting up with her. Somehow that led to a conversation about Benjamin and his operation, which in turn led to a conversation about how crazy Nina was for running away, which in turn led to a conversation about Zoey and Lucas . . . and then they'd bumped into Kate, who had been coming down Leeward Drive from Jake's house—and running into her had incited this really philosophical dialogue about what it was like to be the new person on Chatham Island.

Basically they'd spent the whole day talking about everyone and everything *but* each other and their relationship.

It hadn't been all bad, Christopher had to admit. Talking to Eesh certainly felt natural and comfortable and right. But he wasn't about to forgive her for what had happened the night before—no matter what she thought this day together meant.

"Hey, Eesh, I think I'm gonna bolt," he mumbled. He stood up and stretched. "I'm getting hungry. I'm gonna head home."

"You can come eat up at my place," Aisha suggested quietly. "My parents would love to see you. Kalif would, too—"

"I don't think that's a good idea," Christopher interrupted. He glanced down at her.

Aisha swallowed. "Christopher, please don't start getting mad again," she whispered.

All at once rage engulfed him. Where did she get off telling him not to get mad? He kicked at the sand violently. "Why the hell not? You oughtta *thank* me for the way I've been acting today."

"I know, it's j-just—I can't," she stammered. "I can't. . . ."

"You can't *what?*" he barked. "You can't decide on which guy you want, so you just take them both?"

A pained expression crossed her face. "Christopher, please don't."

"Don't worry, I *won't.* I've made your decision easy for you. You can have David. I won't be around anymore to get in your way." He shook his head disgustedly. "No more surprise visits."

Her head jerked up. "What do you mean?"

"I mean I'm leaving Chatham Island for good in about three weeks," he stated evenly.

"But I thought you just got a job at Passmores'!" she cried.

He shook his head, then turned back to the ocean. "That's only temporary," he muttered. He kept his eyes pinned to the horizon. It would be best not to look at her. That way, he wouldn't have to be constantly reminded of how gorgeous she was, with her long brown curls flowing over the smooth skin of her shoulders, and her bare legs in the sand. . . .

"I don't get it," she said in a trembling voice. "I thought you were coming back for good."

"Yeah, well, you thought wrong. I'm only here to make enough money so I can move to Boston."

"Boston? Wha-what's in Boston?"

He laughed once. "What's here?" He began pacing agitatedly across the beach.

Aisha jumped up and chased after him. "*I'm* here," she said, grabbing his arm. "I need you, Christopher."

"You *need* me." He shook her hand loose. "You sure have a funny way of showing it."

"But what about today?" she cried.

He whirled to face her. "What about it?" he spat. "Don't get any illusions, Eesh. It was nice talking to you. But it's over. This is it. I can't forgive you anymore. It's a waste of time, for the both of us." His voice cracked as he spit out the words.

"But I forgave you," she pleaded. "Remember? I forgave *you*."

Christopher's jaw clenched tightly shut. Why did she have to bring *that* little indiscretion up? He knew he was as guilty of lying and infidelity as she was—but that wasn't the point. It had happened last fall. He had given up chasing other girls a long time ago, and he had never thought about it since.

"That's true," he hissed. "But that was before I asked you to marry me, remember?"

Aisha's face fell. She didn't say anything.

He turned away again. The hurt in her eyes stung him—which in turn only made him angrier. Why should he even care?

"Look, Eesh, it doesn't matter anymore," he said. "It's all in the past. We both just have to get on with our lives."

A lone tear fell from her cheek.

"I don't want to get on with my life if it doesn't involve you," she said.

He shrugged. "You should have thought of that when I asked you to marry me." Then he turned and marched across the sand, thinking only of how much he wanted to shut himself away in Lucas's room and not have to deal with anyone for the rest of the night.

Lucas put the last dish in the oversized industrial dishwasher, then looked at his fingers. They looked like shriveled white prunes.

"Dishpan hands," Mr. Passmore said, grinning. "Don't worry. It's nothing permanent."

"I hope not." Lucas forced himself to smile back, but he felt as if he were about to keel over. He'd never realized how exhausting this kind of work was. How could Mr. Passmore manage to stay so cheerful and energetic the whole time—especially under the circumstances? His coffee must have been loaded with extra-powerful caffeine or something.

"You know, Lucas, you don't have to stick around

if you don't want to," he said. "The afternoon rush is over."

Lucas hesitated. He wanted nothing more than to go home and collapse into bed for about fifteen hours. But he couldn't tell if Mr. Passmore was just being polite. "Um, are you sure?"

"Absolutely." A crooked smile formed on Mr. Passmore's lips. "No offense, but I don't think you'd do me much good, anyway. You look like you're gonna drop dead at any second."

Lucas sighed gratefully. "Yeah, I guess so. Thanks a lot, Mr. P." He untied the white apron Mr. Passmore had lent him and hung it up on a hook by the back door.

"Thank *you,* Lucas. I really, really appreciate all your help." Mr. Passmore reached into his pocket for his wallet, then removed three slightly crumpled twenty-dollar bills. "Cash," he said, handing the money to Lucas with a wink. "This way, you don't have to declare it on your tax returns. Although you didn't hear that from *me.*"

Lucas stared at the money, feeling mildly bewildered. "Uh . . . don't you think this is a little generous?"

Mr. Passmore raised his eyebrows. "Are you kidding? That's not even . . ." His voice trailed off suddenly. "Wait. You hear something?"

Lucas listened for a moment. There were faint shrieks of laughter and excited squeals coming from inside the restaurant.

All at once Zoey burst into the kitchen.

"Mr. Geiger and Mrs. Mendel are getting married next weekend!" she cried. "They're here right now with Claire and Aaron. Come on! Grab some champagne. Mr. Geiger wants to make a toast!"

She disappeared back through the swinging door.

Mr. Passmore glanced at Lucas. "You know, I was looking for an excuse to start partying," he remarked dryly. He reached into a cabinet above the refrigerator, grabbed a couple of large black bottles, then followed Zoey into the restaurant.

Lucas didn't move. He was too tired. So . . . Mr. Geiger and Mrs. Mendel were getting married. Great. He was almost tempted to just slip out the back door and go home—but he knew Zoey would kill him. The very last thing he wanted to do right now was plaster a big fake smile on his face to go out and greet Aaron the Slimeball. He looked longingly at the rear exit, but finally he forced his tired legs to march through the swinging door.

"A round of drinks for everyone!" Mr. Geiger was shouting.

Lucas moaned. The restaurant was in complete chaos. Everybody was screaming and talking at once, and Mr. Passmore was popping the corks off the bottles and passing around glasses, and even total strangers who just happened to be there were clapping. Lucas had a faint feeling of déjà vu. Hadn't they already been through this once before at New Year's Eve?

Zoey appeared at his side and handed him a glass. "Wow," she murmured, surveying the scene. "Pretty crazy, huh?"

"Yeah." He stared at Mr. Geiger, who had gathered Aaron, Claire, *and* Mrs. Mendel into his arms and was squeezing them so hard, he looked as if he might strangle them. "I've never seen Mr. Geiger look so giddy."

"I think it's sweet," Zoey said.

"Mmmm," Lucas grumbled. *Sweet* wasn't the first word that leaped to mind.

"You know what they say about weddings, don't you?" Zoey murmured.

"What's that?"

"You might end up meeting your future spouse there."

"Oh." Lucas felt blood rushing to his face. He sniffed the champagne quickly. He never liked the taste of this stuff—but at this moment a nice little buzz would probably feel good. He threw his head back and drained half the glass in one gulp.

"Whoa, there." Zoey nudged him teasingly. "You better slow down. One alcohol-induced nightmare per day is about all we can handle here."

Lucas laughed. "Don't remind me," he mumbled. "Hey—did you know your dad gave me sixty bucks?" He shook his head, then downed the rest of the champagne. "I can't believe it. I should work here every Sunday."

Zoey slipped her arm around his waist. "You deserve it," she whispered. She kissed him lightly on the cheek.

Lucas smiled. In spite of his exhaustion, he was beginning to feel better fast. The champagne had immediately filled his stomach with a pleasant warmth. His eyes wandered over to Aaron. The guy was looking even more pleased with himself than usual. At least the alcohol took the edge off Lucas's ever present desire to punch him in the face.

"Hey, guys," Claire called, making her way through the crowd to where Lucas and Zoey were standing. "Sorry to spring this on your parents without any warning."

Zoey laughed. "What are you talking about? My dad's always looking for an excuse to come out of the kitchen and establish contact with the outside world. Congratulations, by the way."

"Thanks." She cast a slightly bemused glance at Lucas. "Speaking of the kitchen—was that *you* I saw coming out of there?"

"Yeah," he said. He averted his eyes, mostly because the champagne was making him notice how amazingly sexy Claire looked in her black dress. "Lara wasn't in much of a condition to work today. Actually she wasn't in much of a condition to stand."

"Oh, no." Claire shook her head. "What happened?"

Zoey groaned. "Can we talk about something else, please?"

"Actually, yes," Claire said. She abruptly shifted to her usual cool, businesslike manner. "Nina called. She's coming home tomorrow."

"Really?" Zoey cried. "What did she say?"

"Not much. She's in Boston. She's staying at some place called the Malibu Hotel." Claire shrugged, then flashed a polite smile. "Well, I should probably go mix and mingle."

Yes, you probably should, Lucas thought. He couldn't help but smirk as he watched Claire maneuver her way back to her father. She was so poised, so gracious. Everyone was sneaking a peek at her. Claire lived for moments like this. Even when her own father was supposed to be the center of attention, she always managed to steal the spotlight.

"She sounds thrilled that Nina's coming home, doesn't she?" Zoey whispered sarcastically.

"Nina's probably the last thing on her mind right now," Lucas whispered back. He wasn't so psyched about Nina's return, either—but for purely selfish reasons. He was glad Nina was okay. But when she arrived, he knew she would end up dominating Zoey's life for the next few days. And that pretty much meant Lucas would be left to sit by himself and twiddle his thumbs.

"I wonder why she went to Boston?" Zoey said.

"Who knows? Maybe—"

There was a tap on his shoulder. He turned around. Kate was standing next to him.

"Hey! I didn't even see you come in."

"Yeah, it's pretty crazy here," she said softly.

Lucas took a closer look at her. Her expression seemed far away and distraught. Suddenly he realized how odd it was that she had even shown up here in the first place. "Are you okay?" he asked.

She smiled halfheartedly. "I've been better."

"What's up?"

Her eyes flashed to Zoey, then back to him. "Um, it's just that I, uh, went to see Jake, and, uh . . ."

"I'm going to see if my father needs any help with anything," Zoey said quickly, removing her arm from Lucas's waist. "I'll see you guys in a minute."

The mild euphoria Lucas had experienced after chugging the champagne swiftly evaporated. Why was Kate coming to *him* to talk about Jake? Couldn't she see that he hated this kind of thing? Besides, he wasn't exactly Jake's best buddy. Their relationship was tenuous at best—more of a truce than a friendship.

"Jake wouldn't even talk to me, Lucas," Kate moaned. "What am I going to do?"

Try leaving me the hell out of it, he thought, but he held his tongue. "Um, Kate, why don't you just tell him about Lara, okay? Wouldn't that make things a lot easier?"

"No way," Kate said adamantly. "I'm not going to give her what she wants. Why do you even think she got drunk again this morning? She's begging for people to notice her."

Lucas frowned. "How did you find out about this morning?" he asked.

"I ran into Christopher and Aisha. They told me all about it. So when I couldn't find you at home or at Zoey's, I figured you were probably here."

Great, Lucas thought wretchedly. *You chased me all over town just to drag me into something that doesn't even concern me.*

"Lucas, what am I going to do?" she asked again.

Lucas just looked at her. He had no idea what she was going to do. But he did know one thing. Either she had to work out her problems with Jake, or he had to find another place to live.

Nine

The first sensation Lara McAvoy experienced when she opened her eyes was one of raw, throbbing pain. It seemed as if a miniature jackhammer was pulverizing the area of her brain right behind her forehead. A desperate thirst consumed her. She tried to lick her lips, but her tongue was too dry.

"Oh, God," she croaked.

What was happening to her?

Gradually, in pieces, she became conscious of her predicament: She was in bed. She was in her apartment. The room was dark. Night had fallen. Most obviously, she knew she was suffering from one of the worst hangovers she'd had in a while. But she couldn't seem to remember how she had managed to end up with it.

What's the last thing I remember? she asked herself, feeling as if she were performing a familiar ritual.

Seemingly disjointed images floated through her mind. She remembered sitting on her rug, drinking vodka and orange juice as the sun came up. She also remembered driving by herself at night and shouting at the top of her lungs. Somehow she knew those two episodes were related, but she couldn't figure out how.

After some intense concentration she recalled something else as well: anger. Yes, she was angry; she was angry at Jake. He'd lied to her about the prom. He'd told her he wasn't going, and then she'd found out he was taking that stupid bitch Kate. And then she'd gone out and stolen that bottle of vodka from the Passmores' restaurant.

Gut-wrenching nausea seized her. For a horrible, dizzying moment she felt as if she were about to throw up—but then the feeling passed, leaving only the pain in her head and the cottony dryness in her mouth. She rolled over onto her back.

Why did Jake lie? I don't get it. Why couldn't he just tell me the truth?

She could understand his supposed need to distance himself from her now that he was trying to straighten himself up. It was a phase—but she could understand it. The phase would pass. Sooner or later Jake would realize that a nice, stiff drink every now and then would do him a world of good. She knew him too well. The only thing she couldn't understand was his dishonesty.

If Jake had felt compelled to take Kate to the prom because Kate wasn't a drinker, he should have just told her. She would have understood.

After a couple of deep breaths Lara managed to sit up in bed. She could see the shadowy silhouette of the vodka bottle on the table by the window. It wasn't empty, she realized. A couple of quick swigs would take care of her thirst and her headache—and then she could focus on the important things, like trying to figure out what the hell was going on.

The glowing red numbers on the digital clock by her bed read 9:02 P.M. That didn't seem right. Why would she be waking up *now?* Her clock had probably stopped or gotten unplugged. Judging from the way she felt, it was definitely closer to five or six in the morning. She must have gotten so wasted that she'd passed out really early. But that was okay. After all, she had to go to work in a few hours. She would just have one last drink, sleep off the hangover—and then she'd be in prime form for a day at the restaurant.

All at once the phone started ringing. The piercing noise sounded like an alarm going off in her eardrum. Who would be calling at this hour? She fumbled for the phone, then snatched it off the receiver.

"Hello?" she managed hoarsely.

"So I didn't wake you."

Lara frowned. It was her father. He sounded pissed. What right did he have to disturb her in the middle of the night? "As a matter of fact, you did," she said.

"Sorry, Lara," he snapped. "But we need to talk. Now."

Lara shook her head. She heard voices in the background at the other end—lots of them. Wherever he was, he was with a bunch of people. It sounded like he was at a party, as a matter of fact. Jeff Passmore, at a late-night party? She almost grinned. Was he drunk or stoned or something?

"Your behavior has been . . . well, intolerable," he said. "I'm going to have to fire you."

"What?" she cried. She shook her head uncomprehendingly. "What do you mean? Why?"

There was a pause. "Why?" he repeated. "Well,

101

Lara, I'll tell you. This may come as a shock, but we restaurant owners tend to get a little miffed when one of our employees shows up to work an hour late and then proceeds to vomit all over the kitchen."

At the mention of the word *vomit*, Lara felt as if she might throw up again. Suddenly she wasn't disoriented anymore. Suddenly she was overcome with a terrible, dawning suspicion. She looked at her clock again in the darkness. The glowing numbers now read 9:03. "What—what time is it?" she gasped.

Mr. Passmore sighed. "A little past nine, Lara." His tone softened. "So I gather you don't remember what happened this morning."

"No." Lara's heart began pounding violently. "What . . . ?"

"You came to work drunk. My wife brought you home, Lara. I cleaned up your vomit, and my wife brought you home. Ring any bells?"

"Oh, God." Lara closed her eyes, but dizziness forced her to open them again quickly. What had she done? It wasn't Sunday morning; it was Sunday *night*. Since when had she blacked out for so long?

"And no, Lara—you don't have to thank us or apologize," Mr. Passmore barked. "I wasn't expecting as much."

"Wait a minute," Lara begged desperately. She rubbed her forehead with her free hand, struggling to think. "I mean, I'm sorry, but I just don't know. . . . I, uh, I'm really fired?"

"Yes, Lara, you're fired," Mr. Passmore replied. "But once again, I will repeat what I've been telling you all along. As soon as you're ready to take responsibility for what you've done and ask for

102

help, we'll be here for you. Until then, you'll have to manage things on your own."

She shook her head. She hated that condescending, paternal tone he was always taking. All of a sudden she found she was furious. "How am I going to manage things if I don't have a job?" she shouted.

"You should have thought of *that* before you got drunk this morning, Lara," Mr. Passmore shot back.

Before she could reply, there was a loud snap in her ear.

"Hello?" she yelled. "Hello?"

But there was no answer. He had hung up on her.

Lara slammed the phone back on the hook and sat for moment, looking wildly around the shadowy room. *This must be some kind of nightmare,* she thought. *This can't be happening. . . .*

How could her own father keep doing this to her? How could he invite her to live with his family, only to kick her out of his house? How could he offer her a job, only to take it away from her without warning?

Okay, so she had screwed up a little; she could admit that. But he never once let her have a second chance. Come to think of it, nobody did. Her father was just like Jake: He had dumped her without a thought.

She was all alone.

For some reason, the words Jake had said to her at that New Year's Eve party came drifting through her memory. *"You can trust me, Lara. That's the truth. And you can trust the Passmores, too. . . . No one here is out to get you."*

Lies, she realized. *All lies.* She couldn't trust anyone. Why had she ever been so stupid to believe that she could have?

Well, there was nothing she could do about it now. The only thing left to do was unscrew the cap of that vodka and raise a toast to her solitude.

It was nearly eleven by the time Zoey staggered home with her parents, feeling burned out, haggard, and slightly drunk. She marched immediately upstairs to her room and fell facedown on her bed. She couldn't believe she actually had to go to school tomorrow. She felt as if she could sleep until Tuesday. First the prom, then the Geiger champagne fest.

It had been pretty fun, she had to admit. Once the celebration had gotten started, there was no stopping it. It seemed as if everyone had to make just one more toast. The party just kept going, and going, and going. . . .

Just like the Energizer Bunny, Zoey thought fuzzily. She giggled at her own dumb joke. *Uh-oh.* She was glad nobody could see her. Unfortunately she was fully aware that alcohol turned Zoey Passmore into an embarrassing drip.

She yawned. The only sour part of the evening, of course, had been Lucas's mood. Once Kate had left, he'd spent the next two hours moaning and groaning about how much he hated having to listen to other people's problems. He should have taken his own advice. He'd even suggested that he sneak over tonight and sleep at her house—in Benjamin's room, of course. She smiled. Yeah, right. She probably would have had to bar her door with cement blocks and a padlock.

"Hey, Zoey," her father called from downstairs. "We got a message from Benjamin."

Zoey immediately rolled over and sat up. "What did he say?"

"Not a whole lot. He's in Boston. Apparently Nina's there, too, somewhere. He's staying at that place he stayed when he went down with her that time—the Malibu Hotel."

The Malibu Hotel? Zoey gasped. She bolted out of her room to the head of the stairs. "Are you sure?" she asked.

Her father shrugged. "That's what the message said."

"Dad—*Nina* is staying at the Malibu Hotel. Claire told me tonight."

Mr. Passmore's jaw dropped. "Are you serious?"

"Absolutely." Zoey bounded down the steps and rushed past him to the kitchen phone. "We have to call him! I mean, can you imagine?"

Mrs. Passmore was sitting at the table in the breakfast nook, drinking a glass of water. "He didn't leave a number, Zo," she said, staring as Zoey grabbed the phone.

"We'll call information," Zoey said, undeterred. "Boston has a six-one-seven area code, right?" She glanced at her mother, who was smiling at her with one of those "you-are-totally-insane" looks. Zoey turned back to the phone and grabbed a pen. "Yes, operator? I'd like the number for the Malibu Hotel, please." She scribbled down the seven digits and hung up. "Isn't this great?" she cried.

Mr. Passmore walked into the kitchen and leaned against the counter. "Maybe he already bumped into her," he suggested quietly.

Zoey frowned. She glanced back and forth between her parents, who were looking at each other with those thoughtful, knowing expressions they sometimes got. "Oh, boy," she said, rolling her eyes. "You aren't going to try to tell me that I shouldn't call, are you?"

"Zoey—Benjamin's gone all this way to find Nina on his own," Mrs. Passmore said. "He's almost there. I don't know if we should spoil it for him."

"Spoil it for him?" Zoey yelled. "By telling him where Nina is? That's the whole *point!*" She shook her head. "That's the dumbest thing I ever heard, Mom."

"Not really, Zo," her father said patiently. "Your mother has a very good point. I mean, just think about it for a sec. We all know how depressed Benjamin has been these past few months. This is the first time he's done anything on his own in a long time—anything that calls for total self-sufficiency. It's really the first time he's behaved like the old Benjamin since the operation. And I think that success for him now, without any interference on our part, will do wonders for his self-esteem."

Zoey paused. Her hand was on the phone. She could see his point, sort of. . . . But still, what if Benjamin didn't run into Nina? Wouldn't that be *more* frustrating? Wouldn't it be more of a failure if he came home only to discover that Nina had been staying in the same *building?*

"I'm going to call him," she announced. She hastily punched in the number before either of her parents could protest any further.

"Good evening, Malibu Hotel," a cheery male voice answered.

"Yes, hello, could I please be connected to Benjamin Passmore's room?"

"One moment, please." There was a click, followed by a few seconds of silence, then with another ring.

"Hello?" Benjamin's sleepy voice answered.

"Hey—I didn't wake you up, did I?"

"Not really," he said. At once he sounded much more alert. "What's up, Zo? Is everything all right?"

"Everything's great," Zoey said, unable to keep from smiling. "I just thought you might like to know that somebody I know is staying at the Malibu Hotel, too. You might want to look her up while you're there. Her name is Nina Geiger."

"Oh, my God," Benjamin breathed. "You're kidding."

Zoey laughed. "Nope."

"Did you talk to her?"

"No. She called Claire this afternoon to let her know she was fine and that she was coming home tomorrow. Mr. Geiger and Mrs. Mendel are getting married next weekend, by the way."

"Wow." Benjamin didn't say anything for a moment. "Any other exciting news I should know about?"

Zoey almost blurted out that Lara had been fired—but she stopped herself at the last second. Now would probably not be the best time to bring that up. "Uh . . . no."

"Claire didn't say what room Nina was in, did she?" Benjamin asked.

"No, she didn't."

"Hmmm. Well, I'll figure it out. . . ." He ended the sentence on an uncertain note, as if he'd wanted to say something else.

"What is it?" Zoey asked.

"Um, put Mom and Dad on, too—will you, Zo?"

"Uh, sure," she said. She glanced over her shoulder at her parents, both of whom were gazing at her expectantly. "Benjamin wants to talk to you, too."

"Just put it on speaker," her father instructed.

Zoey pressed the speaker button, then hung up. "Benjamin, can you hear us?" Mr. Passmore called.

"Yeah." Benjamin's voice sounded small and far away. "Listen, I have something to tell you—and I want you all to promise me you won't panic or anything."

Zoey shot a frightened glance at her father. He blinked, but his face remained calm. "Go ahead," he said.

"I've had these two little flashes of light. It was just like what I saw when I got my bandages off. First there was pain, and then there was a flash, then nothing. And I thought I could see other things as well—fuzzy shapes and things."

Zoey's stomach jumped. She stared at the phone in shock. How could Benjamin sound so relaxed about this?

"When did this happen?" Mr. Passmore asked.

"Once this morning, and once about an hour ago."

"I see." Mr. Passmore marched across the floor and picked up the phone. "Benjamin, I want you to stay at that hotel, okay? I'll come down tomorrow and—" He began shaking his head rapidly. "No, I am *not* panicking. I just want to be there with you when we go pay Dr. Martin a visit. Which we're going to do the moment I get there."

"Dad, I can handle this on—"

Mr. Passmore shook his head again. "The answer is *no*, Benjamin," he stated firmly. "I pay your doctor's bills, remember?" He looked around the room and rolled his eyes. "No. I'll catch an early bus and be there no later than two. Just sit tight. Give my best to Nina when you see her, and tell her we're all happy she's coming home. Bye." He hung up the phone.

"Is he going to wait for you?" Mrs. Passmore asked anxiously.

"Yeah, he'll wait." Mr. Passmore ran a hand through his long hair. "Well, the old Benjamin is definitely back." He laughed tiredly. "He kept telling me not to bother coming down and that I was overreacting."

Zoey sat down at the table in a haze. "What . . . what do you think it means?"

"I have no idea," her father said. "But you can bet I'm going to find out."

Nina

Graduation? Oh, sure, I can't wait. As of graduation day, I will officially become Weymouth High's Biggest Loser. Queen of the Dweebs. Her Royal Lameness. Right now, the title belongs to some other lucky senior who has absolutely no friends. But soon I will ascend to the throne! I think the coronation ceremony usually follows the valedictorian address.

I'm not offering this information because I'm fishing for compliments or sympathy or anything like that. I don't

want people to say, "But, oh,
Nina, you'll have plenty of
friends!" Because the truth is
I will have <u>no</u> friends. Not
one. It's not any kind of
exaggeration. It's a simple
statement of fact.

You see, throughout my
illustrious career at Weymouth
High, I've always hung out
with people a grade ahead of
me. I know, I know—I
wasn't exactly planning ahead.
But foresight has never been
my strong suit.

So what does this mean?
Well, graduation marks the day
when each and every one of
my friends walks out of my

life. I mean, admittedly, I'm not the most popular girl in school to begin with. But there are a few people who at least acknowledge my existence: namely Zoey and Aisha. Even Jake and Lucas aren't so bad. I can even deal with the Ice Queen of the Underworld (that is, my loving older sister, Claire) when I have to.

But they're all graduating. It's pretty astounding when you think about it. There might as well be a clause in their diplomas that states: "You are now wiping the vile stain of Nina Geiger clean from your lives for all eternity. Salutations."

I don't think I'm overreacting. Let me explain why. Have you ever seen a movie about a high-school reunion? No. Of course not. That's because high-school friends don't keep in touch. But there are plenty of movies about college reunions—because, as everyone knows, wacky college buddies stay friends for life.

Oh, yeah, that's another thing I can look forward to: future holidays when Zoey and Eesh bring all their new wacky college buddies home to visit.

And Benjamin is graduating,

too, of course. But what do I care about that? It's only proper that The Empress of All Losers should have a heartless ex-boyfriend. I can also look forward to the day when he returns to Chatham Island with a stunning, sophisticated, brilliant girl from New York City . . . one who will probably look a whole lot like Kate Levin. Maybe they'll even get married.

So you see, I'm really excited about graduation.

Ten

"Come on, Mary," the fat, balding guy in the bad suit was saying to Mary Tyler Moore. "Come on. . . ."

"But Mr. Grant!" she cried.

The laugh track cut in.

Nina made a face. There were people on this planet who actually *liked* this show? Maybe. The ex–cast members probably liked it.

Nina had been lying in bed for hours, watching one cheesy seventies sitcom after another. The only light in the room was the harsh, flickering glow of the TV. She felt as if she were part of a weird *Twilight Zone* episode. *Girl mysteriously gets beamed back to era of polyester bell-bottoms. All at once, cast of* Rhoda *bursts in and tortures her to death with New York accents.*

With a bare minimum of movement Nina picked up the remote control and began flipping through the channels. News. Sports highlights. *Beavis and Butt-head.* A cooking show. She let her hand drop. Watching an old bearded man stir a pot of borscht for a few minutes would certainly be enough to lull her to sleep.

Or maybe it wouldn't.

Unfortunately, guilt had done a pretty good job of

keeping her awake so far. Her father had called about an hour ago, bubbling with the news about the impending wedding. Occasionally he would try to act serious and say that he and Nina had "some important issues to work out"—but mostly he just giggled. For some reason, that made her feel even worse.

Why had she even run away in the first place? It had been so idiotic. Benjamin certainly wasn't worth all this trouble. He probably hadn't even noticed she was missing. In all likelihood, the only people who were truly aware of her absence were her teachers.

Maybe she would end up flunking and have to repeat the eleventh grade. Or maybe she would just be expelled for excessive truancy. That would lead to a pretty interesting state of affairs, she realized. One Geiger sister would go on to win the Nobel Prize for some amazing scientific discovery about clouds—while the other, a high-school dropout, would go on to do something like work in a shoelace factory or become a topless roller-skating waitress.

She turned up the volume on the TV. What was Claire even doing right now? She was probably in the kitchen with Aaron, the midget, and Mr. Geiger, working out the details of the wedding. Or for all Nina knew, Claire could have gotten back together with Benjamin. Maybe the two of them were taking a moonlit stroll on the streets of North Harbor. Or maybe she had brought him up to the widow's walk to initiate him into her coven. . . .

Nina shook her head. She needed to stop thinking, period. Thinking was getting her nowhere.

Benjamin sat on the edge of his bed, wishing desperately that he had brought his Discman with him. Some good music would help him to relax right now. But he'd packed in such a frenzied haste that he hadn't been thinking. He'd only thought of getting to Nina. And now it looked as if his trip was going to last even longer than expected.

He tapped his feet agitatedly on the floor. Telling his family about the flashes had been a good idea; he realized that now. He was actually relieved that his father had decided to come here. He had to admit he was scared. And he didn't want to face this alone.

His thoughts wandered back to Nina. She was *here.* She was in this very building—maybe even on the same floor, maybe even in the next room, 212. But secretly Benjamin prayed she wasn't. Secretly Benjamin wished she was on the fourth floor, in a very specific room.

If Nina was in room 428, it was a good sign. It might mean she had been drawn to this place out of love—out of a shining memory of that night they had spent together. And if that were the case . . . well, he supposed he still had a chance. Obviously he was still on her mind. But had she come here to say one final good-bye to her past before she shut him out of her life for good? Had she come here out of spite? It was a very distinct possibility. He had given her every reason to feel spiteful.

There was only one way to find out. He stood up and reached for his cane. His legs were trembling, as if they were made of liquid. But he forced himself to walk to the door. And at that moment Benjamin realized something: He was far more fearful of facing Nina than he was of the bizarre flashes of light and pain in his eyes.

This chef must be on drugs, Nina thought with a sneer. How could anyone possibly get so excited over a bowl of soup? True, she liked a nice gazpacho as much as the next person—but this guy did a fervent little jig every time he took a taste, then howled in ecstasy. Of course, if she were getting paid to go on TV with soup recipes, she might very well howl, too.

She glanced at the clock. It was almost eleven-thirty. All this talk about soup was making her hungry. She would watch until twelve, then order some room service, then go to sleep. No—she would order the room service now, then watch more TV in bed while she ate. Why not be as decadent as possible? She only had one more night of easy living. She picked up the phone and pressed for the front desk.

"Can I help you?" the man at the other end asked.

"Yeah," Nina replied. "Do you have room service?"

He laughed. "What are you, kidding?"

"Of course I'm kidding," Nina growled. "This is an in-house crank call."

The guy laughed again. "Look, if you're really hungry, there's a deli down the block that delivers. Tell me what you want and I'll call it in for you."

"That's more like it. I'll take a roast beef on whole wheat bread with lettuce, tomato, and mayo. And a diet Coke. And some chips."

There were some scribbling noises, then the guy said, "What room are you in?"

"Four twenty-eight," she replied. "My name's Nina."

"All right, Nina. One roast beef sandwich coming up."

"Thanks a lot." She hung up the phone.

The bearded man on TV was still ranting about gazpacho, so Nina pressed the mute button and began flipping through the channels again. There had to be something better than a cooking show. But most of the good channels were probably blocked out. The Malibu Hotel wasn't exactly the kind of place that indulged its patrons with such luxuries as HBO.

Come to think of it, the Malibu Hotel was totally lame. She was probably making a huge mistake letting that guy downstairs order for her. The odds were she would wind up getting tuna on a hard roll and a gallon of whole milk. If the food ever came at all.

About a minute later there was a knock on the door.

"Coming," she called. Wow. That had been pretty fast. Actually that had been *really* fast. Maybe the sandwich was one of those premade jobs that had been sitting around in some dark refrigerator for the past eight years. She jumped out of bed, walked across the room, and threw open the door.

"Oh, my *God!*" she shrieked.

"I was hoping you'd be here," Benjamin choked out. The sound of Nina's voice, combined with the familiar scent of coconut shampoo and tobacco . . . it was almost too much for him to handle. He was

119

nearly overwhelmed by the urge to throw his arms out in the blackness and pull her against him. But he knew he couldn't.

"What . . . wh-what are you doing here?" she stammered.

He swallowed. "I was, uh, just in the neighborhood. I figured I'd drop by," he said quietly.

She didn't respond. He heard no movement, not even the sound of her breathing. There was only silence. His face began to grow hot. Had he made a terrible mistake? Was it too late? After a minute he cleared his throat. "I was hoping you'd at least compliment me on my glasses," he mumbled.

There was a sniffling sound. "Oh, God, Benjamin," she sobbed. "Why did you come here?"

The pain in her question was too much. It released a flood of hot, salty tears—a furious stream that poured down his cheeks.

"I love you," he whispered after a moment. His voice was tremulous. "And I always have. That's why I came here. That's why I knew you were in this room."

She didn't speak right away.

"But what about what you said in Miami?" she finally murmured. "What about Kate?"

Benjamin shook his head confusedly. "Kate?"

"I saw you kiss her, Benjamin. Don't deny it."

All at once he realized what she was talking about: the night Kate had thrown herself at him, thinking he was some chivalrous mystery man, a gallant rescuer—a guy who actually turned out to be Jake. Jake McRoyan, aka Sir Galahad. It was completely absurd. Benjamin suddenly found that he was giggling through his tears.

She sniffed. "What's so funny?"

"Uh, Kate thought I was someone else," Benjamin explained.

"How could she think you were someone else?" Nina cried. "*You're* the one who's blind!"

"She thought I was the guy who took care of her when she was unconscious. It was so stupid. She thought I was Jake because I was wearing his shirt."

"You were wearing Jake's shirt?" she asked, totally flabbergasted. All at once she started laughing hopelessly. "Benjamin, that's the most idiotic excuse I've ever heard!"

"Then you know it's true," Benjamin said in dead earnest. He took a step forward. "Nina, how could I ever care about anyone but you? I've been chasing after you for days now. I followed you to Portsmouth and asked around at all the—"

"You went to Portsmouth?" she gasped.

"Yes. And then, by pure luck, I just happened to run into this guy Niko who worked at a Greek restaurant, and he told me he had seen you and that you were coming here. He even drove me to the bus station."

"Wow," Nina breathed. "I . . . I don't believe it."

"It's true," Benjamin said.

Nina didn't say anything for a long, long time.

Finally Benjamin straightened and wiped his face with his palm. "So here I am."

"Oh, Benjamin . . ."

He felt the familiar arms wrap around him, that familiar body press tightly against his own, those familiar lips kiss his neck. How could he have ever let this go? He didn't even know he could feel so good, so complete. The tears kept running down his face—but these were tears of happiness. He ran his fingers through her hair and luxuriated in the soft, silky feel. "I love you so much," he murmured. "I'm so sorry, Nina. You don't know how sorry I am."

"I'm so happy you chased me," she whispered, squeezing him tightly. "I'm so happy—"

Without warning, the searing pain in his eyes struck again.

He staggered backward and cried out, tearing the glasses off his face. But this time the pain didn't recede.

"Benjamin, what's wrong?" Nina shrieked, grabbing his shoulders.

"My eyes . . ." He pressed his palms against them, barely aware that he had fallen to his knees. Nina's fingernails dug into his flesh.

"What is it?" she pleaded.

He just shook his head. *Why is this happening to me?* he demanded silently. *Why . . . ?*

After an agonizing few seconds the pain began to fade.

Benjamin remained still. Sweat dampened his forehead. Slowly he took his hands away from his face. His eyelids were still squeezed shut. He hadn't seen the bright light yet, but he was certain he would.

"Benjamin?" Nina whispered.

He took a deep breath and held it in his lungs. Then he blinked. He blinked again. His pulse started racing. There was no flash—but there was *something.*

A fuzzy, oval-shaped object.

He opened his eyes as far as he could. The light from the blurred image stung his pupils for a moment, but he didn't care.

He was *seeing.*

Gradually, second by second, the image in front

of him came into focus. Every other sense, every tool on which he'd relied for the past seven years . . . all of it melted into nothingness. He no longer smelled; he no longer heard; he no longer felt. He only *saw.*

And then he realized what he was seeing.

It was a face.

Benjamin was consumed with wonder. It was a delicate, narrow face, framed with black hair. Its cheeks were glistening. The face belonged to a girl: a girl with gorgeous red lips and a little nose—and the most stunning gray eyes he ever remembered seeing. He almost thought he was hallucinating. But this was more real than any of his dreams or memories had ever been.

"It's beautiful," he whispered.

"Benjamin?" the face asked.

And then he smiled. "Nina? Oh, my God—Nina, is that really *you?*"

"What?" she murmured uncomprehendingly.

"Nina, I can *see* you!" He reached forward and grabbed her hands. He held them up to his eyes, afraid to blink for fear they would vanish before him. He could see the tiny fingers he knew so well by touch and smell; he could see those purple fingernails about which he had heard so much over the years. He laughed wildly. "Nina—I can really see you!"

A wide, bewildered smile formed on her lips. She began shaking her head. "Benjamin . . . Benjamin, th-this—this is," she sputtered. "Oh, my God!"

"I know!" he cried, unable to control himself. "Nina, you're beautiful! You're so beautiful. . . ."

All at once Nina's head jerked up to her left.

Benjamin turned.

A slightly out-of-focus man was standing before them. Benjamin squinted at him. He was holding something—a crumpled bag.

"Everything all right here?" he asked in a thick New England accent.

Benjamin nodded. He stared at the man, absorbing every wrinkle of his craggy face, every brown wisp of hair on his balding head, every item of oversized clothing on his fat body: his rumpled white T-shirt and blue jeans. It was amazing, all of it.

"Nina?" the man asked.

"That's me," Nina said.

"Good. That'll be seven-fifty." The man frowned at Benjamin. "I guess you're pretty hungry, huh, champ?"

Benjamin had no idea what the guy was talking about. But he didn't care. He just kept staring. "Why?" he finally asked.

"'Cause I gotta be honest with you," the man said. "I don't think I've ever seen anybody so excited to see roast beef on wheat in my whole life."

Eleven

The Wild Week Before the Wedding

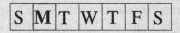

Monday morning, Nina arrived in Weymouth. Mr. Geiger met her at the bus station. He told her that they still had to talk about the "Truth or Dare stunt" she pulled with Claire. Since Nina had no idea what her father was talking about, she told him about Benjamin. Just as she'd anticipated, he promptly forgot about the "Truth or Dare stunt"— whatever *that* meant.

Monday afternoon, Benjamin laid eyes on his father for the first time in seven years. After a tearful embrace at the bus station they proceeded directly to Boston General to see Dr. Martin. The doctor was cautious in his prognosis and warned that Benjamin could still have a long road to full recovery. He insisted that Benjamin remain at the hospital under observation until Friday. Despite much protest from Benjamin, Mr. Passmore insisted on staying as well.

Monday night, Zoey received a call from Lara, who drunkenly blamed her for getting fired. Zoey tried to reason with her, then finally hung up, with Lara still screaming in her ear.

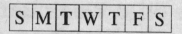

Tuesday morning, Claire woke up early and sneaked into Nina's room to instruct her on how to handle the Truth or Dare issue. Nina fell asleep several times during the lecture. Finally Claire wrote the story down in detail on a piece of paper and taped it to Nina's forehead.

Tuesday afternoon, Jake went to baseball practice. Kate was waiting for him with her camera. Amid hoots and catcalls from his teammates, Jake angrily asked her to leave. Kate told him that she only wanted to take pictures. Jake said she had no business taking his picture without his permission. Finally Kate stormed off, leaving Jake feeling very confused and very miserable.

Tuesday night, Zoey called Lucas and insisted that he tell Jake what really happened the night of the prom. She admitted that Lara was beginning to frighten her. Lucas promised her that he'd talk to Kate.

| S | M | T | W | T | F | S |

Wednesday morning, Christopher accused Lucas of using up all the toothpaste. Lucas very calmly told him that he had every right to use up the toothpaste; it was *his* bathroom, in *his* house. Christopher told him to shut up. Lucas told him to find a new place to live.

Wednesday afternoon, Aisha summoned the courage to call Christopher after school. Christopher curtly told her that he was busy trying to find a permanent apartment. Aisha offered to put him up at Gray House. Christopher responded by hanging up the phone.

Wednesday night, Zoey talked to Benjamin and her father in Boston. Apparently Benjamin's vision was improving each day. He was experiencing occasional headaches and blurriness of vision, but Dr. Martin felt hopeful that these would recede in time.

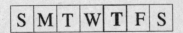

| S | M | T | W | T | F | S |

Thursday morning, Lara discovered she had run out of cash. Since she didn't feel like going all the way to the bank in Weymouth, she came up with an easier solution. She still had the key to Passmores'. After a rousing breakfast of several Bloody Mary's, she let herself into the restaurant, opened the register, took four twenty-dollar bills, and fled.

Thursday afternoon, Lucas returned home from school to find Kate in tears. He tried to console her but gave up when Kate still refused to tell Jake about Lara.

Thursday night, Zoey discovered that money was missing from the register in the restaurant. She immediately panicked, but her mother told her not to jump to any conclusions. They would discuss the theft when her father got home.

Later, Zoey left a message on Lara's machine stating that if Lara ever stole from the restaurant again, Zoey would call the police and have her thrown in prison.

Deep Thoughts on the
Impending Union
of Burke Geiger and
Sarah Mendel

Nina

What do I think? I
haven't had any time to think
about anything except how
I'm going to make up all the
schoolwork I missed. Oh, yeah:
one thought. Sarah should
wear platform shoes at the
ceremony—you know, like the
ones the members of Kiss wear
in concert. Otherwise she
might have to stand on a
stack of telephone books to
kiss my dad.

Claire

Thoughts on the wedding? Weather permitting, the exchange of vows will take place at 4 p.m. on the church lawn, with a reception to follow at Gray House. What I'm trying to say is that I've been so busy planning the wedding that I really haven't had time to think about its long-term implications. Or maybe I just don't want to think too hard about the fact that Aaron is going to be my brother.

Aisha

What do I care? I hate weddings. If I had it my way, they'd get married in Bali.

Unfortunately the reception is taking place at my house.

Zoey

I think that the new Geiger family is going to have some tough times ahead. After all, Nina and Claire call their future stepmother "the midget." And the relationship between Aaron and Claire is . . . interesting, to say the least. I guess the only thing I can do is wish them good luck. They're going to need it.

BENJAMIN

I'm just glad I'm actually going to see the wedding. Is Sarah Mendel really as short as everyone says she is?

LUCAS

I'm using the reception as an opportunity to slip poison to certain guests— namely Aaron Mendel, Kate Levin, and Jake McRoyan.

JAKE

To be honest, I'm a little nervous about the whole thing. There's a lot of booze at weddings. I just hope they serve sparkling cider.

Christopher

THE WEDDING? YEAH. WEDDINGS SUCK. AND THERE'S NO WAY I'M GOING TO THE RECEPTION.

Friday

6:13 a.m.

After blowing half her money on the water taxi, Lara staggers home from a wild night in Weymouth. She listens to the one message on her machine, then passes out on the floor.

7:05 a.m.

Nina finally apologizes for the letter and explains that "Truth or Dare" is a game that Claire invented—mostly to get boys to take their clothes off. She enjoys the rest of the meal in silence.

7:40 a.m.

As the ferry pulls out of North Harbor, Aisha seeks out Lucas below deck and demands to know why he is kicking Christopher out of his house. Lucas tiredly tells her that Christopher is staying. He contemplates throwing himself overboard.

8:05 a.m.

The ferry arrives in Weymouth. In icy tones Claire thanks Nina for going along with her story.

9:45 a.m.

Dr. Martin tells Mr. Passmore and Benjamin that Benjamin is free to go home. He'll need to return for more tests in the next few months, but right now the best thing for him is rest and relaxation.

11:04 a.m.

After spending the entire morning thumbing through the classifieds of the *Boston Globe*, Christopher realizes his chances of finding work in Boston are pretty grim. He decides to take the next ferry to Weymouth and look for work there.

12:20 p.m.

Jake approaches Lucas at lunch and asks him if Kate really got a flat tire the night of the prom. Lucas tells him not only did she get a flat tire, but the car went into a ditch, and Mr. Cabral had to get it out, and that Kate has been driving him crazy for the past week. Then he tells Jake to leave him alone.

1:07 p.m.

Lara wakes up, immediately pours herself a vodka and orange juice, and listens to Zoey's message again. After playing it several times, she hurls the answering machine against the wall.

2:39 p.m.

After a fruitless search for work, Christopher wanders by the old pawn shop where he bought Aisha's ring. He decides to go in and buy Mr. Geiger and Mrs. Mendel a wedding gift.

3:15 p.m.

Aaron surprises Claire by showing up at school to meet her. Unable to control herself, Claire embraces him passionately—much to the amusement of Nina, who makes gagging noises. The two of them decide that they must finally tell their parents about their involvement.

3:45 p.m.

Zoey and Nina arrive at the bus station to meet Benjamin and Mr. Passmore. Benjamin bursts into tears when he sees them.

3:47 p.m.

After frantically pacing in front of the pawn shop for over an hour, Christopher decides to buy another ring. He finds a plain silver band identical to the last one he bought. Lucas was right; he *is* frustrated about Aisha. He's going to forgive her one last time. He's going to give her one last chance to make it right.

3:57 p.m.

Lucas and Jake board the ferry. Claire and Aaron are on deck making out, so the two of them head to the cabin below. Neither acknowledges the other's existence.

4:00 p.m.

Christopher makes the ferry at the very last possible second. Suddenly he realizes he forgot to buy Mr. Geiger and Mrs. Mendel a wedding present.

4:45 p.m.

Lucas arrives home to find Kate sitting on the living-room couch, somberly looking through her photos of Jake. He decides to loiter on Zoey's front walk until she gets home.

6:09 p.m.

Lara finishes the bottle of vodka and opens a new one. She decides to have one more drink before she pays Zoey Passmore a visit. . . .

Twelve

"You know what the most incredible thing is?" Benjamin said, pausing on Dock Street in front of the restaurant. "Everything and everyone here looks exactly how I remember."

Zoey just smiled. She hadn't been able to take her eyes off him as they took the ferry home. He looked so different, so *changed*. It wasn't the absence of his ever present Ray-Ban sunglasses or the beautiful brown of his eyes that she was so unaccustomed to seeing. It was the look on his face—the expression of childlike wonder, of pure joy. He even walked differently: faster, as if he wanted to make up for all the years he had been afraid to run.

"I don't know if that's good or bad," Nina said with a smile.

"I don't know if it's even *true*," Mr. Passmore added. "I've added a lot more gray hairs in the past seven years. And I've lost a bunch of my old ones. I think you're being polite."

Benjamin cocked an eyebrow. "Don't flatter yourself, Dad."

"Hey," Zoey said, nudging him. "You think Nina and I want to hear that we look like little kids?"

"Seriously," Nina said. "I had major blubber going on when I was nine."

"Well, there's only one person I can think of who looks exactly the same—and that's your mother," Mr. Passmore said. "Prepare yourself to be dazzled by the ageless wonder."

"Wait!" Zoey blurted. "Let me just run home and get a camera. It'll take two seconds."

Benjamin rolled his eyes. "Zoey, that will take all the spontaneity out of it."

"Yeah, it'll look just like a still from a really cheap made-for-TV movie," Nina added. "The 'homecoming' shot."

But Zoey was already running toward South Street. "You guys are so unsentimental!" she shouted. The Passmores had never made a big deal out of taking photographs—for obvious reasons. In fact, the last time Zoey could remember snapping a picture was before Benjamin went blind. But now it was time to start a new tradition. Even the time of day seemed to call for it: The early evening sun cast everything in a beautiful, radiant golden hue. Now was the perfect time.

As she turned onto Camden she saw Lucas sitting on her front step. "Hey!" she called breathlessly. "Benjamin's home!"

He stood up and gave her a lazy smile. "Cool. I could use some cheering up."

"What's up?" she asked. "What are you doing here?"

"Waiting for you," he said, catching her and kissing her lightly on the lips. "And escaping the torture of the Cabral household."

"Well, you can forget about all that for now," Zoey said, pulling him into the house. "Benjamin is dying to see you. He's dying to see everyone, as a matter of fact. I just wanted to find the camera. We're all gonna have a big celebratory dinner down at the restaurant."

"There seem to be a lot of big celebratory dinners these days," Lucas mused.

Zoey dashed up the stairs. "I'll just be a sec. I think it's in my parents' room. . . ." She rummaged through the bottom drawer of her father's desk. There it was—an old Polaroid Instamatic. She grabbed it and laughed out loud. This would be perfect. They wouldn't even have to wait for the pictures to be developed.

"Hey, Lucas," she said, bounding back down to the first floor. "Don't you think—"

She broke off when she saw Lucas staring out the front door.

"What are you . . . ?" She gasped. "Oh, no."

Lara was stumbling up Camden Street toward the house.

She was totally disheveled—her hair was unkempt and her shirt hanging out of her pants. Even from where Zoey was standing, she could see the dark circles that ringed Lara's eyes.

"Let's just get out of here," Zoey whispered. She took Lucas's arm, marched outside, then locked the front door behind her.

"Hold on!" Lara shouted. "Don't even try it. You're not going anywhere."

Zoey felt Lucas stiffen as Lara approached. There was no mistaking the odor that wafted toward them.

"We gotta talk," Lara said, planting herself precariously in front of them. Her mouth hung open limply.

"There's nothing to talk about," Zoey muttered, brushing past her. "So get lost."

"You'd like that, wouldn't you!" Lara shouted after them. "You'd like that! Well, it's not gonna happen!"

Zoey forced herself to keep walking. She refused to turn around. She was not going to indulge Lara. She was not going to be intimidated by her. She was not going to let her ruin Benjamin's night. Besides, Zoey had done more for Lara than anyone realized; she'd kept her promise to Lucas not to tell about what Lara had done to Jake. Not to mention the fact that Lara had basically gotten away with robbery.

"Don't you think we should talk to her?" Lucas breathed. "I don't know if it's such a good idea to leave her like this."

"She'll handle herself," Zoey said firmly. "She always does."

Claire had been jittery ever since she'd gotten home from school. But now, as she prepared to go to Passmores' with Aaron, Mrs. Mendel, and her father, she could actually feel sweat on her palms. She couldn't ever remember that happening before. For some reason the old cool, confident Claire Geiger had disappeared this past week. The new Claire was a little frightening.

"I think we should tell them now," Aaron hissed in her ear as her father closed the door behind them.

She nodded, then trotted down the front steps. Now would be the best time; she knew that. It had gone on long enough, and something was bound to slip out sooner or later. After all, their involvement was no secret among her friends—which probably meant it was no longer a secret among her friends' parents, either. She could just picture Mr. McRoyan

140

making some totally inappropriate comment about "the two happy couples"—which would send Mrs. Mendel into the kind of frenzy Claire had seen on Sunday.

"You know, this is so nice," Mrs. Mendel said with a sigh. "There's so much to celebrate tonight."

Mr. Geiger slipped his arm around Mrs. Mendel's waist as they strolled leisurely down Lighthouse Road. Absently Claire moved farther away from Aaron. She looked out across the bay at the lights of Weymouth, glittering in the fading sunlight. *Maybe now isn't the best time to tell them,* she thought glumly. *Maybe we should save it until after the ceremony. In fact, maybe we should wait another ten years.*

"Which reminds me, we still have a few things to settle about the event tomorrow," Mr. Geiger said. He winked at Mrs. Mendel. "We seem to have made a small oversight. We still haven't picked out a maid of honor or best man yet."

Claire shot a glance at Aaron, who just shook his head. So much for the confession. There was no way they could possibly tell them *now*—not when they were about to get all sentimental and gooey.

Mrs. Mendel laughed. It was that high-pitched squeak that still grated on Claire's nerves and probably would for the rest of her life. "So if you two aren't doing anything . . ."

"Well, what about Nina?" Claire found herself asking. "I mean, uh, don't you think she'll feel left out?"

Mr. Geiger gave her a skeptical smile. "That's thoughtful of you, Claire. But you know how Nina is. She dreads these kinds of things. It'll be a big enough task to convince her to be in the wedding party at all—just as a bridesmaid. Besides, she has so much on her mind right now with Benjamin."

"Plus you did so much to help us this week, Claire," Mrs. Mendel said. "You deserve it."

Claire plastered what she hoped was a grateful smile on her face. *You wouldn't think that if you knew I was fooling around with your son.* "Uh . . . thanks," she said.

"Now, all this means is that you'll have to stand next to us when we exchange the vows," Mr. Geiger said. "And make a toast at the reception, of course. . . ."

Claire tuned her father out as they crossed the dock area. The restaurant was right in front of them. It was now or never. She kept stealing furtive looks at Aaron, who was smiling and nodding but probably equally as far away from the conversation as she was.

Suddenly Aaron stopped walking. Mr. Geiger paused.

"Uh, look, before we go in," Aaron began quietly, "there's something I just want to say to both of you."

Claire froze.

"It's just that Claire and I are . . . well, we're . . . we're very happy for the both of you."

"Aw, honey . . ." Mrs. Mendel rushed over and threw her arms around him.

Claire let out a deep sigh. But she couldn't tell if it was in relief, or disgust, or both. All she could think was: *Nice job, Aaron. We're never going to tell them, are we?* Her eyes met Aaron's as Mr. Geiger clapped him on the shoulder.

"So much for coming clean," he mouthed silently.

Nina tried to maintain the big, fake smile on her face, but her cheeks were starting to hurt. "If Zoey doesn't put that camera away soon, I'm going to have to smash it over her head," she murmured in Benjamin's ear.

"If I don't first," Benjamin whispered back.

For the past fifteen minutes Zoey had been running around the table, snapping away like a madwoman, hooting with delight every time a blurred, overexposed image formed on the film. So far they'd amassed about a dozen horrible shots of Nina, Benjamin, and his parents—looking alternately phony or exasperated.

"Just one more," Zoey promised. She frowned at Benjamin. "Come on, one more smile, okay?"

"Hey, uh, Zo?" Lucas mumbled. "Maybe we should take a rest, huh? Benjamin's probably exhausted."

For once in her life, Nina actually felt sorry for Lucas. He'd been standing off to the side, smiling awkwardly—completely overwhelmed by the way Zoey was freaking out.

"Hey, Lucas," Nina said. "Why don't you take one last picture of all of us—including Zoey?"

Zoey looked doubtful. "Well, I don't know if I really feel like having my picture taken. . . ."

Nina rolled her eyes.

"That's a great idea," Lucas said. He snatched the camera away from Zoey. "No arguments. Everyone get together and say cheese, all right?"

Zoey reluctantly stood behind her parents. Nina put her arm around Benjamin. She squeezed close to him as she stared at Lucas. He was fumbling with the camera.

"I, uh, just push the button, right?" he asked.

Nina started laughing. "Lucas, if you don't take this picture soon, I'm going to have to kill you."

"Hey—look!" Zoey suddenly cried. She rushed over to Lucas and grabbed the camera. "Wait, wait. We have to get a shot of the bride- and groom-to-be."

Nina swiveled around to see her father strolling in with Mrs. Mendel, followed by Claire and Aaron. *Here come the beautiful people,* she thought wryly. Everyone in her family and family-to-be was always making her feel so underdressed. It seemed as if her father looked for any excuse to wear a three-piece suit. And Claire, in her own way, was exactly the same. She was wearing a dark blue dress that hugged every curve on her tall, slender body.

"Hey, congratulations!" Benjamin called.

Mr. Geiger strolled over and clasped Benjamin's hand. "Congratulations to you, too, Benjamin. I'm so happy for you."

Claire began making her way to the table. A shy smile curled on her lips.

Suddenly Nina realized that Benjamin hadn't seen Claire yet.

Her stomach turned. So *that's* why Claire was so dressed up. She wanted to make an impression on her ex-boyfriend. She looked beautiful. . . . No, she looked *more* than beautiful. She looked resplendent. Dazzling. Goddesslike. Nina held her breath.

"Hi, Benjamin," Claire said.

Nina's eyes flashed between them. Claire was staring down at him adoringly—almost seductively. *She wants a reaction,* Nina thought, grinding her teeth. *She wants Benjamin to stumble for a second, to be overwhelmed by her. She wants him to see*

144

what he lost when he decided to give up on her and go out with me.

But Benjamin just gave her the same easygoing grin he had given Mr. Geiger. "Hey, Claire," he said, shaking her hand. "It's good to finally see you after all these years." He turned back toward the table.

A fleeting but triumphant relief flashed through her.

He hadn't swooned; he hadn't blinked. Not even Claire's undeniable beauty could stir any old passion he might have felt. Those feelings had died.

He was truly hers.

She'd known it all along—but here was the final proof. Benjamin had gotten his sight back, and he *still* loved her. Zoey had been right.

Sorry, Claire, she said to herself.

For an instant Claire's expression faltered. At the exact same moment her face was lit up with the harsh glow of a flashbulb.

"Gotcha!" Zoey cried happily.

Nina smirked. The picture was already sliding out of the camera. Claire made a face, but Zoey didn't seem to notice.

"This is great," Zoey said, shaking the photo and squinting at it. "I think I got everyone." She walked over to the table and handed it to Benjamin.

Nina leaned over Benjamin's shoulder and stared at the photo intently. Gradually the faces appeared: Aaron's, Claire's, her own, Benjamin's, Mrs. Mendel's, Mr. Geiger's, the Passmores' . . . and everyone was smiling. Everyone but Claire. Her lips were perfectly horizontal. Her eyes were on Benjamin, and her face was blank.

"Uh-oh," Benjamin muttered. He started giggling. "The flash does something to the eyes."

Nina peered at the photograph. It was true; everybody's eyes were glowing bright red. And then she decided to say something she knew she would regret—but she couldn't help herself. The moment was too perfect.

"See, Claire!" she exclaimed. "You really *do* look like Satan!"

Thirteen

Friday nights were always the hardest, Jake realized. That was because for as long as he could remember, Friday night always held so much promise. When he had been going out with Zoey, it was the night they spent together—alone. When he had been drinking, it signaled the beginning of a long, wild weekend. But now . . . now, Friday night was just empty. There was nothing to do.

He paced anxiously around his room, glancing at his reflection in the darkened windows. He considered going to Passmores'; he wanted to see Benjamin, after all. His parents were on their way there right now. But he just didn't think he could deal with so many people—especially Kate. Besides, he knew he would see all of them tomorrow at the wedding.

Would Lara be at the wedding, too?

She'd been on his mind more than once in the past week. He knew she'd been fired—which meant that she had probably been drinking more than usual. His eyes wandered to the painting he still kept above his desk, the portrait she had painted of him in January. Even now it provoked a reaction. It was almost as if it made him see things within himself that he didn't know existed: kindness, but sadness as well.

He shook his head angrily. If Lara had so much talent, why was she always screwing up? Why wasn't she making the most of her abilities? It was such a stupid waste. There was no telling what Lara could do if she straightened herself out. She could be . . . well, she could be like Kate. Talented, beautiful, and sophisticated. She could be anything she wanted, if it weren't for her alcoholism.

Just then the phone rang. He picked it up.

"Hello?"

"Jakee!" the familiar, drunken voice shrieked in his ear.

He closed his eyes for a moment. "Lara," he breathed. "I was just thinking about you."

There was a loud giggle. "That's funny," she said. Her words were slightly slurred. "I was just thinkin' about *you.*"

He frowned. "Where are you right now?"

"I'm at . . . I'm at my dad's." She hiccuped. "Where are you?"

"I'm at home," he barked. "You called *me,* remember?"

"Oh, yeah." She laughed again.

Jake's eyes narrowed. "Wait a second—did you just say you were at your dad's?"

"Mm-hmmm. You know what, Jakee? I think I'm in big, big trouble."

A sickeningly familiar despair engulfed him. "What did you do, Lara?"

"Well, you see . . ." She took a deep breath. "Zoey wouldn't let me in. So I kinda—I kinda had to smash one of the windows. Y'know, just to—"

"You broke one of the windows?" Jake interrupted.

She let out a cackle. "Thass juss the start, Jakee. That's just—"

Jake pressed the hook, silencing her. Then he released it. The moment he heard the dial tone, he furiously punched in the number at Passmores'.

Come on, he silently urged. *Come on, pick up.*

Finally after five rings there was a click. "Hello?" Mr. Passmore asked.

"Mr. Passmore, this is Jake. Listen—"

"Jake!" Mr. Passmore exclaimed. "Where are you? You're missing all the fun. Your parents just got here. Why don't you come on down?"

Jake swallowed. "Lara is at your house, Mr. P. I think she might have broken something. She just called here—"

"Whoa, whoa, whoa," Mr. Passmore interrupted. "Slow down, Jake. What's going on?"

"Lara just broke into your house. You better go there."

There was a brief pause. "What did she say?"

"She said she broke a window," Jake answered quickly. "After that I hung up and called you."

"Dammit," Mr. Passmore mumbled. "Look—do me a favor, all right? Meet me there as soon as you can."

"I will."

"Thanks a lot, Jake. I owe you one." The line went dead.

Jake hung up the phone. His hands were shaking. In fact, his whole body was shaking. He glanced at the painting. Suddenly he tore it off the wall and hurled it to the floor. Then he dashed out into the night.

Benjamin stared as his father burst through the swinging kitchen door. His face looked deathly pale.

"What is it?" Benjamin asked. The crowded restaurant fell silent.

"Lara," Mr. Passmore muttered. He marched for the exit. "Look, everyone just stay here. This shouldn't take long."

At the mention of his half sister's name Benjamin immediately stood up. He hadn't even *thought* of Lara in the past week. But now he was suddenly filled with curiosity. "Where is she?"

Mr. Passmore stopped at the door. "Our house."

"What?" Zoey yelled. She leaped from her chair. "That's impossible! I locked the door."

"Jake just called," Mr. Passmore said, with obvious impatience. "She broke a window or something. I'll be back in a few minutes." He shut the door behind him.

The assembled throng began to buzz with muted conversation. Benjamin shot a look at Zoey. The two of them simultaneously bolted for the door.

"Benjamin!" Nina called after him.

He glanced over his shoulder. "I'll be right back."

The next thing he knew, he was chasing his father down the moonlit cobblestone streets of North Harbor, with Zoey at his side.

I must be dreaming, he thought. The moment was too surreal. He wasn't yet used to seeing the sidewalks speeding past underneath his feet when he moved. It gave him a strange and dizzying sensation. Still, he almost felt as if he were twelve again— before he got sick, before he had gone blind. He could imagine he was a boy, racing his little sister back home. The white picket fences and shingled houses that bordered South Street were exactly as he recalled them. Nothing had changed. Only the intensity of his nervousness kept him grounded in the present.

"Lucas told me not to leave her there," Zoey said, pulling ahead of him as they turned onto Camden. "I should have listened. . . ."

Benjamin slowed to a walk. His house was there: its lights ablaze behind a shroud of drawn curtains. His eyes roved over the second floor with its sloping roof—the three dormered windows and brick chimney in the middle. It was the house of his childhood. How many hundreds of thousands of times had he walked these exact steps in darkness? He couldn't even remember the feeling. In darkness he had always pictured the vision exactly as he was seeing it before him at this moment. But he had forgotten how bright everything could be, how vivid all the colors were: the green of the lawns, the yellow of the daffodils by the front walk.

Mr. Passmore was standing at the door. "What are you two doing here?" he hissed. "Go back to the restaurant!"

"I kinda wanted to see Lara for myself," Benjamin said quietly, pausing with Zoey on the steps.

Mr. Passmore stared at the two of them for a moment. "All right," he said reluctantly. "But prepare yourself for the worst." He jerked a finger at one of the living-room windows. Half of it lay in shattered pieces in the bushes in front of the house. Benjamin swallowed.

Mr. Passmore shoved a key into the lock, then slowly pushed open the door. "Lara?" he called. "Lara, are you here?"

Benjamin heard footsteps pounding up the street behind him. He turned around to see a short, stocky figure with wiry brown hair dashing toward the house. Benjamin squinted into the shadows.

"I got here as fast as I could," the figure gasped. He froze when he met Benjamin's gaze.

"Jake?" Benjamin asked. He smiled slowly.

"Oh, man," Jake whispered. He shook his head with an apologetic grin. "I totally forgot. It's, uh, good to see you, Benjamin."

Benjamin blinked. "It's good to see you, too."

"I guess you heard—"

"Shhh!" Mr. Passmore hissed.

Benjamin shrugged, then turned and followed his father into the front hall. He tried to concentrate on the gravity of the situation, but he couldn't. Seeing Jake confirmed what he had already secretly been thinking ever since he had arrived: He really *had* been the Blind Wonder. Everyone looked exactly how he had envisioned them—down to the hair hanging in Lucas's eyes, the cold smile on Claire's face . . . and now the baggy sweatpants Jake was wearing. Only Nina looked more stunning than he could have imagined. She was the only one who had surprised him.

"Lara?" Mr. Passmore called again.

Benjamin looked over his father's shoulder into the living room. "Oh, no. . . ."

A thin girl with short blond hair—Lara, obviously—was lying facedown on the carpet. The room was a shambles. The couch was overturned; paintings were torn and strewn about the floor; broken vases and plants were scattered over every possible surface. A pungent mixed scent of dirt, sweat, and alcohol filled the air.

"I don't believe it," Mr. Passmore muttered. He strode across the room and lifted Lara's listless body into his arms. She moaned in response, but her eyelids remained closed.

Benjamin glanced at Zoey. He was speechless.

Zoey just shook her head. Her face was twisted in worry and disgust and disbelief. "Well, Benjamin, I guess there's only one thing left to say," she finally stated. Her voice was trembling. "Welcome home."

Fourteen

"Mom, can't I stop now?" Aisha's little brother whined. "This room looks ready to *me*."

Aisha rolled her eyes at her mother, who was placing wineglasses at one of the tables they had set up in the living room of the bed-and-breakfast.

"All right, Kalif," Mrs. Gray said. "Thanks for your help."

Kalif grinned, then bolted out into the foyer and upstairs.

"*What* help?" Aisha muttered.

Mrs. Gray smiled. "He did his part. Anyway, he was doing more harm than good. He kept putting the spoons on the wrong side of the plates." She put the last glass down and surveyed the scene with satisfaction. "Looks pretty good, if I do say so myself."

Aisha nodded. It was true: The house looked as if it had been transformed into some four-star restaurant. The circular tables that filled the living room and dining room were draped with beautiful white linen tablecloths and covered with china place settings. A vase of flowers sat at the center of each one.

"I guess all that's left are the place cards," Mrs. Gray said.

"I'll put those out, Mom," Aisha said.

Mrs. Gray looked at her dubiously. "You sure?"

Aisha nodded. "Yeah." The truth was that the chore of preparing their house for the reception had kept her mind occupied, off other things—namely Christopher. She wanted to keep busy. If she didn't, she was worried she was going to start slipping into a deep, deep depression.

Mrs. Gray sighed. "Well, thanks, honey. I guess I'll just follow Kalif upstairs, then. I want to get a good night's sleep. We've still got a lot of work to do tomorrow."

Aisha tried to smile. "Good night, Mom."

"Good night." Mrs. Gray paused in the foyer. "Honey—are you all right?"

"Fine." Aisha nodded quickly. "I'm just tired, I guess."

"Hmmm." Mrs. Gray sounded doubtful. "Are you still planning on going down to Passmores'?"

"Maybe. I'll call up to you if I do."

"Okay." She smiled. "Good night."

Aisha heard her mother's footsteps plodding up the stairs. At least her mother didn't keep bugging her until Aisha finally told her what was wrong. She laughed wretchedly. *Nothing's wrong, Mom. It's just that I lost Christopher forever. Besides that, everything's peachy.*

She was just about to head to the kitchen to fill out all the name cards when she heard a tap on the window. She frowned.

"Who is it?" she whispered, squinting at the glass. The glare of the lights inside made it difficult to see anything but her own reflection.

"Christopher," came the muffled reply.

Aisha's eyes widened. "Christopher?" she gasped. "Hold on." She immediately dashed for the door and flung it open.

He walked toward her across the lawn. She blinked several times. She almost felt as if she couldn't trust her eyes; after all, the last time she had even spoken to him, he had hung up on her. But he was *here*. Her eyes flashed over his body from head to toe—his sneakers, his jeans, his T-shirt, his windbreaker rustling in the cool night breeze . . . and finally his gorgeous, chiseled face and soft brown eyes. "What are you doing here?" she whispered.

He glanced inside the door. "Uh, can you come outside for a minute?"

"Sure," she said, bewildered. She closed the door behind her and walked with him across the lawn toward Climbing Way. The Weymouth harbor blinked at them from across the water.

For a moment she was too nervous to speak. There was no sound except for the wind and the steady chirping of crickets. Christopher walked slowly, his hands in his pockets. His eyes were focused on the ground in front of him. She tried to read his expression, but she couldn't. It wasn't angry, but . . . sad? Confused? Upset?

"So I guess you're pretty busy planning for the big reception tomorrow, huh?" he asked casually.

"Uh, yeah." She tried to swallow. "It's kind of fun, actually."

He nodded. "Are you going down to see Benjamin later?"

"I haven't decided yet." She looked at him, then looked away. "I guess I just figured I'd see him tomorrow. . . ."

"That's kind of what I figured, too." He smiled. "Although to tell you the truth, I was kind of thinking of blowing off the wedding. I've still got to find a place to live. . . ."

Aisha was confused. "But . . . uh, you're going to Boston tomorrow?"

Christopher stopped walking and took a deep breath. "No. I'm staying here."

Aisha froze. Her heart was suddenly thumping loudly. "You are?"

"Yes, I am." He stepped forward and looked into her eyes. "Aisha, I've been doing a lot of thinking today, and . . . and I realize that everything I said in the past still holds true."

She bit her lip. "What do you mean?"

His face softened. "I mean that you were right. You forgave me—and now I forgive you. The only reason I've been so upset . . . that I've been so angry is that I still love you." His lips twisted into an ironic little grin. "I've been such a jerk because I love you so much. Does that make any sense?"

Her eyes moistened. "Oh, Christopher . . ." She threw her arms around him and buried her face in his neck. "It makes perfect sense. It really does."

He stepped apart from her and took her hands. "Now, Eesh, I have to know something," he said, very seriously. "I have to know if you meant what you said on the beach the other day. You know, that you don't want to get on with your life if it doesn't involve me?"

"Of course I meant it," Aisha breathed.

"Good." He let her hands drop, then reached into his windbreaker pocket, pulling out a small velvet box.

Aisha stared at the box, then looked deeply into

his eyes. Yes, this was the man with whom she wanted to spend the rest of her life. She knew that now. She wasn't terrified or shocked—unlike the last time this had happened. She was just elated.

"I know this setting isn't as romantic as La Cocina Della Fontana, but it will have to do," he said. "Aisha Gray, will you marry me?"

"Yes, Christopher Shupe," she replied unflinchingly. "I'll marry you."

A dazzling smile lit up his face—and immediately he embraced her, kissing her passionately on the lips.

"Wait, wait," she said, laughing. He kept a tight grip around her waist. "There's only one thing. This is important."

He raised his eyebrows. "What's that?"

"It's going to have to be a long engagement," she replied firmly.

"Hmmm." He tilted his head. "How long are we talking about?"

"Four years."

"Four years!" he cried. "Eesh, that's—"

"Shhh," she whispered, placing a finger gently over his lips. "Christopher—I'm *yours*. That's final. And when I put this ring on, that's my way of telling the world that I'm going to marry Christopher Shupe. I just want to wait until I graduate from college. That's what I should have told you the first time you asked me."

He shook his head. "But why? What difference does it make?"

"Because that's the way I feel. I want to have college behind me when I become your wife. At that point I'll be in my twenties, I'll have a degree . . . I'll be able to truly consider myself an adult. Until then, I can't."

"But you're an adult *now,* Eesh," he protested.

"No," she said carefully. "I'm not. But I'm old enough to know that you're the only man for me." She smiled and pulled his face close to hers, so that their foreheads and noses were touching. "And I'm gonna be damn proud to tell the world that you're my fiancé," she breathed.

His brow grew furrowed. She knew he was turning her words around in his head, weighing them for all they were worth. Finally he nodded. "I guess if that's how it's gonna be, that's how it's gonna be."

"Good." She kissed him once, then stuck out her hand. "Now put this ring on and we'll go tell my parents."

By the time the last bit of spilled plant soil had been vacuumed from the rug, Zoey felt as if she were going to explode. She and Jake had been cleaning up the aftermath of Lara's rampage for the past hour while Lara had been taking a nice snooze in Benjamin's bed. Zoey couldn't believe it. Lara had singlehandedly ruined Benjamin's homecoming. At least Benjamin had agreed to go back to the restaurant to try to enjoy himself. But there was no way he could dispel the sour pall that had been cast across his night.

Zoey shut off the vacuum and wheeled it back to the front hall closet. Upstairs, her father was talking animatedly on the phone. She couldn't hear exactly what he was saying, but hopefully he was talking to the police—or the insane asylum.

She cast a glance over her shoulder at Jake, who was straightening a painting on the living-room wall. *Poor Jake.* What was he even doing here?

"Jake, thank you so much," she called. "You don't have to hang around and help me clean up, you know."

He turned around and shrugged. "I really have nothing better to do," he said simply.

"Why don't you go down to the restaurant?" she suggested. She collapsed onto the living-room couch and cast a quick, critical glance over the area. Apart from the absence of all the items that Lara had destroyed—and the hole in the window—the place was actually starting to look habitable again. Fortunately Lara had passed out before she could wreak havoc in any other parts of the house.

"I, uh, really don't feel like it," Jake mumbled distractedly. He sat down on the couch next to her. "I guess I really don't feel like being around certain people."

Zoey nodded sadly. *Kate,* she said to herself. *He doesn't want to be around Kate because he's still angry at her. He still has no idea of the truth.* She found she was seething with anger. Lara had caused this whole mess. Lara was directly responsible for Jake's misery. She was responsible for Kate's misery as well. *And* Lucas's—because Lucas had to put up with Kate. It was ridiculous. When would it end? How much would Lara be allowed to get away with? It wasn't fair to anyone—least of all Jake.

"What are you thinking?" Jake asked.

"I, uh . . . nothing," she stammered. "I guess I'm just mad." She rubbed her temples, hopelessly wrestling with her thoughts. If she told Jake the truth now, she would be breaking her promise to Lucas. She swore to herself that she would never break any promises to him again. But at the same time Jake had a right to know. And if she told Jake, she would even be *helping* Lucas—because Jake would forgive Kate, and Kate would snap out of her depression. More important, everyone would know the truth. Keeping the secret wasn't getting anyone anywhere.

Jake sighed. "I know this may sound ridiculous right now—but in a way, you were lucky. I mean, at least she passed out. When Lucas and I had to deal with her, she was awake the whole time—puking and cursing us out."

Zoey shook her head. Hearing that settled it. Jake had been tormented by Lara long enough. And now he wasn't even *aware* of it. She turned to him. "Jake, I have something to tell you. And it's . . . it might be hard for you to believe. But I know it's true."

He looked at her apprehensively. "Oh, God. What is it?"

"The reason Kate got a flat tire the night of the prom was because Lara ran her off the road."

Jake blinked a few times. Then his face wrinkled, as if he had just caught a whiff of something rotten. "That's crazy."

"It's true, Jake. I *know* it."

"Why?" he demanded.

"She wanted to keep Kate from going to the prom with you," Zoey said evenly.

Jake paused. "If that's true, why the hell didn't Kate tell *me?*"

"She didn't tell you because she knew that's what Lara wanted. The whole reason Lara did it in the first place was so that you would feel sorry for her."

"Feel sorry for *her?* For trying to kill someone? That doesn't make any sense, Zoey—"

"Exactly. It doesn't make any sense. That's Lara, Jake."

Jake stood up and paced for a moment. "So . . . I mean, Kate was protecting Lara this whole time, right?" he asked. "Why?"

"She wasn't protecting Lara, Jake. She thought she was protecting *you*. She knows you well enough to know how guilty you'd feel if you knew that your ex-girlfriend tried to run your prom date into a ditch."

Jake laughed grimly. "Well, you're right about that."

"But that's not important. The important thing is that it wasn't your fault, Jake," Zoey stated. "And it wasn't Kate's, either. It was Lara's. Lara set out to ruin your prom—and she succeeded. She got exactly what she wanted."

"Oh, jeez." He put his head in his hands. "I can't believe this is happening—"

"It doesn't have to *keep* happening," Zoey pleaded. She stood up and put her arm around him. "Go to Kate now and tell her that you know the truth. Tell her I told you. Tell her I'm sorry—but I thought you finally had a right to know."

Jake let his hands drop to his side. He nodded. "You're right. I mean, I don't even know if she'll even talk to me after the way I treated her all week. . . ."

"She'll understand," Zoey insisted. She heard her father plodding down the stairs. "I'm sure of it."

Mr. Passmore walked into the room. He stopped when he saw Zoey's arm around Jake. "Everything all right?" he asked concernedly.

"Yeah," Zoey replied. She patted Jake on the back. "I think Jake's gonna take off."

Jake nodded. "Yeah." He flashed a grateful smile at her. "Um, thanks, Zo." He headed for the door. "I'm sorry about all this, Mr. P."

"Don't be sorry," Mr. Passmore said. "I can't thank you enough for the way you've helped out tonight."

Jake just shrugged.

"Wait—before you leave . . . you might want to know that Lara's going to be leaving the island tomorrow." Mr. Passmore glanced at Zoey, then back at Jake. "I've just been on the phone with Serenity Hills Clinic, in Portland. They've agreed to accept Lara for the next six weeks."

Zoey let out a huge sigh of relief. All she could think was: *Now nobody else will get hurt.* She looked at Jake. He was nodding thoughtfully.

"Good," Jake said. "She needs all the help she can get."

Mr. Passmore extended a hand. Jake shook it firmly. "Thanks again for everything, Jake," he said. "I guess I won't see you tomorrow—but have fun at the wedding."

"I will. Take care." He gave Zoey another quick smile, then closed the front door behind him.

Mr. Passmore flopped down on the couch. "Wow," he breathed, leaning his head back and closing his eyes. "What a night, huh?"

Zoey sat down beside him. "You did the right thing, Dad," she said. "You really did."

He looked at her out of the corner of his eye and grinned. "Wait a second. Did I actually hear you say that I did something *right?* I might want to get this on videotape."

She laughed quietly. "This is one of those freak

occurrences," she said. "You know, like a total eclipse."

"I'll savor it." Mr. Passmore's smile grew melancholy.

"What is it?"

"It's just—I really tried with her. I really did. . . ."

"You did more than any other person on the planet would do, Dad," Zoey cut in gently. "You have superhuman patience. Why do you think I get so frustrated with you all the time?"

He laughed.

"Anyway, once she gets the help she needs, we can all start over. As a family."

Mr. Passmore leaned over and gave her a hug. "Why do you always make me feel like the luckiest dad on the planet?" he murmured.

"Because you are," she answered. "Speaking of which, what do you say we go back and join Benjamin?"

"Good idea." He stood up. "I don't know about you, but I could use a cold beer right about now."

Fifteen

Lucas squirmed in his chair in the bright afternoon sun. His suit was too tight and too hot. The wedding was dragging on endlessly. Every time he thought that they were getting closer to the "kiss-the-bride" part, somebody else would say something or read something. It was ridiculous. When he and Zoey got married, they were definitely going to keep it short.

His eyes wandered across the crowd of people to where Zoey, Benjamin, and Mrs. Passmore were sitting. Zoey was leaning forward with a rapt, glazed expression on her face. He shook his head. She loved big, sappy occasions like this. Her mind was probably miles away.

His mind, on the other hand, was right here—on her. He still hadn't gotten a chance to speak to her yet. It was driving him crazy. She'd called him this morning and informed him that she had something important to tell him. Then, of course, she had insisted that she could only tell it to him face-to-face.

He could already guess what it was.

She'd told *someone*—Nina or Benjamin or Aisha or maybe even Jake—about what had happened to

Kate on prom night. He shook his head. It was bound to happen, but at this point he really didn't care. He would actually be *relieved* if she had broken her promise to him. As far as he was concerned, anything that would get Jake and Kate back together would be a good thing.

"Does anyone here have any objections to this union?"

Finally, Lucas thought, looking up at Father Donahue, the wizened old priest sandwiched between Mr. Geiger and Mrs. Mendel.

"Speak now or forever hold your peace." Father Donahue poked his head out at the crowd, then smiled. "Then I now pronounce you man and wife. You may kiss the bride."

Lucas glanced over at Zoey again. She was dabbing her eyes with a Kleenex. He grinned. Who else but Zoey Passmore could summon up tears at the sight of Burke Geiger kissing a woman half his size?

I know I'm going to hurl, Nina thought as she watched her father lift the veil off Sarah's face, then bend down to kiss her. Mrs. Mendel was practically standing on her tiptoes. It would have been funny if it weren't so . . . nauseating.

To make matters worse, her sister was giving Aaron this little sexy smile. Nina couldn't believe it. Her father and the dwarf were smooching like they were in a Big Red commercial, and her sister and stepbrother were checking each other out. What kind of a family was she getting herself into?

She knew Claire must have thought Aaron looked really, really hot in his tuxedo. As far as Nina was concerned, he looked like a mafia hit man. He was probably thinking about how he wanted to tear Claire's purple bridesmaid dress as soon as the wedding was over. . . . *Yuck*. She couldn't think about that anymore. It was way too gross.

At least the dresses were purple, she reflected. She could stand there in front of everyone without feeling like a *total* moron. For a while last week she'd been worried that Mrs. Mendel would insist on pink.

Finally, after what seemed like an eternity, the new Mr. and Mrs. Geiger stepped apart. Then Mr. Geiger proceeded to step on a glass wrapped in a handkerchief.

"Mazel tov!" Aaron yelled. A loud cheer erupted from the crowd.

Nina forced herself to clap along with the rest of them, then she fell into line behind Claire and Aaron. It was fitting somehow: Nina was walking alone down the aisle behind the two happy couples. It was all so . . . she immediately tensed when she thought of the word. *Incestuous*.

A strange rush of emotions flowed through her at that moment: sadness, pain—but in the end, relief and gratitude. She knew why her father had kept the wedding parties so small. In part it was the same reason he had probably rushed the wedding in the first place: because he hadn't invited his sister, Elizabeth.

He must have known Aunt Elizabeth's presence would have stirred up a lot of very agonizing memories, even though Elizabeth had long since left Mark. But Nina hadn't seen her aunt since that night last fall—the horrible, frightening night when she'd revealed the truth about what Mark had done. And this was Mr. Geiger's way of demonstrating to Nina that he didn't ever want her to endure something like that again. He knew she had suffered enough.

Her father was really an incredible human being, she realized. He deserved all the happiness in the world. And for the first time since Nina and Claire's mother had died, he was truly content. She knew that he would miss his former wife for the rest of his life—in some ways, maybe even more than his daughters would. But he had been lucky enough to find someone who could provide the love and support and companionship he needed. . . .

Uh-oh, Nina thought quickly. *I'm heading for cheeseville.*

She flashed a look at Benjamin. He was smiling at her. He tilted his head toward Zoey, who was sniffling like a baby. Nina rolled her eyes. He winked.

All at once Nina felt like a snake who had just shed an old skin. The past was crumbling and slipping away—and with it, the pain. Mark would never hurt her again. Her father was starting a new life. And she just had established something: She could now communicate with Benjamin without any words. His eyesight added a new dimension to an already totally complete and fulfilling relationship. It was . . . well, it was beautiful.

As her eyes roamed over the sea of guests she let out a long sigh. Maybe cheeseville wasn't so bad. All in all, things were pretty good—even if she *did* want to hurl every time her father and her new stepmother kissed.

The moment the ceremony ended, Jake leaped out of his chair and immediately made a beeline through the swarm of guests for Kate.

168

"Hey, Jake?" his father was calling after him. "Where are you . . . ?"

Jake ignored him. He couldn't wait to talk to Kate any longer. He still hadn't had a chance to ask her about what Zoey had told him. After he'd left the Passmores' house last night, he'd spent the next hour looking all over North Harbor for her—at the restaurant, on the beach . . . and when he had finally tracked her to the Cabrals', Mr. Cabral had gruffly told him that she had already gone to bed.

He licked his dry lips as he drew closer to her, suddenly gripped with fear. She looked so radiant, with her flowery dress and long red curls, laughing and chatting with Mr. Cabral. What was he even going to say to her?

Mr. Cabral stopped talking when he noticed him approaching. "Hello, Jake," he said shortly. "Well, I'm going to catch up with my wife." He smiled at Kate and hurried toward the throng on Church Street, looking stiff and awkward in his dark suit. Jake watched him. He wondered what feelings Mr. Cabral truly held toward his family. Hatred? Anger? Resentment? He probably felt the same way that Jake had felt toward *him* until Jake had learned the truth about Wade's death and Lucas's role in it. But he couldn't worry about that now. It was in the past. He had to focus on the present.

"Hi, Jake," Kate said shyly. "I was hoping to talk to you." She looked at the grass. "I just wanted to apologize for the way I acted on Tuesday at your baseball practice—"

"That was my fault," Jake interrupted.

She looked up at him.

"I was being a jerk, Kate," he said quietly. "I had

no right to act that way in front of all those people." He swallowed. "You can . . . you can take my picture whenever you want to."

She smiled confusedly. "I was kind of a jerk, too. But thanks."

Jake shifted his weight from one foot to the other. "Look, I'm really, really sorry about the way I've been acting this past week. It was wrong." He looked at her. "If it's okay with you, I'd like to . . . I don't know—do something sometime. Wipe the slate clean and start over."

"Jake . . . ?" she asked slowly. Her gaze intensified. Her eyes seemed to bore into his own. "Did you talk to Lucas by any chance?"

He shook his head.

"Well, let me put it this way," she said. "Did you find out something about Lara?"

Jake hesitated for a moment, then blurted, "Zoey told me what happened, but it was because Lara went—"

"It's okay, Jake," she interrupted softly.

"Please don't be mad at Zoey," Jake said. "I had a right to know."

She looked away. "I know. I should have told you right away. It was just that . . . I guess I wanted revenge. It's so stupid. But the best way to get revenge on someone like Lara is to ignore her completely."

Jake nodded. "I know. I've been there. But the thing is, revenge doesn't work with her. She always gets you back."

Kate looked at him again. "Lucas told me about what happened last night at the Passmores'."

"Yeah, well, I think things are gonna finally settle

down." He sighed. "Mr. Passmore is taking Lara to a rehab clinic right now."

"Wow." She chewed her fingernail absently for a moment. "Well, I guess that's the best thing."

Jake didn't say anything.

Finally, after what seemed like a very long time, Kate smiled—slowly at first, and then more broadly until her whole face seemed to be shining with its own light.

"Well," she said. "Since we both missed out on the prom, I think we're going to have to do our best to make up for it, don't you?"

Sixteen

Lara stared blankly out the window of her father's van as it hurtled along the highway toward the outskirts of Portland. She felt the way she always did when she was hung over: sick and dizzy and thirsty and tired. But today her discomfort was compounded by something else: distress. Apparently it had been decided—by someone other than *she*—that she was no longer capable of being in charge of her own life. And now she was being locked up.

"How are you doing?" Mr. Passmore asked.

She grunted. How did he *think* she was doing? He had taken away her home, her job—and now he was taking her freedom. Oh, yes, she was doing great. Never better. Perfect.

"You know, Lara," he began. "I don't—"

"Don't start," she spat. She whirled around to face him, her puffy, bloodshot eyes blazing. "You have no idea what I'm thinking right now, *Dad*—so just shut up."

He nodded, keeping his eyes on the road. "You're right," he said evenly. "I don't. Why don't you tell me?"

She turned back to the window and snorted. If there was one thing she hated about Jeff Passmore, it was the way he was always affecting that easy-going, you-can't-bother-me-because-I'm-too-mellow attitude. It was such b.s. Obviously he wasn't *that* mellow or else he wouldn't be institutionalizing his own daughter.

"I'll tell you one thing," she muttered. "I could really use a drink right about now."

"Lara, you can stop trying to provoke a reaction," he said dully. "I don't have enough energy to get angry anymore. It's too tiring."

She looked at him again. "Yeah, right," she growled. "I guess that's why you're letting somebody else handle your problems. It's too tiring."

"Lara, if *you* can't handle your problems, how do you expect someone else to?"

She frowned. What the hell was that supposed to mean? "I can handle myself just fine, thanks," she said. "You're the one who's blowing this whole thing way out of proportion."

"Out of proportion," he repeated flatly.

A sneer curled on her lips. "So I guess you aren't as tired as you thought, huh, Dad?"

He shook his head. "Lara, can I ask you something?" His tone was much softer now.

Oh, brother. "What?"

"Why haven't you apologized yet?"

"Apologized?" she cried. "I said I was sorry this morning. Jeez—what do you expect?"

"You said you were sorry for breaking the window," Mr. Passmore said. His voice was colorless, impossible to read.

"Yeah? So?" She waited for him to say something else, but he seemed poised for a response. Finally she sighed. "Okay, I'm also sorry I broke a cheap vase you got at Sears for like five bucks. I told you

I'd pay you back. Besides, I don't even *remember* that part."

"Oh, I get it," he said slowly. "If you don't remember, you aren't responsible."

Anger flashed through her. He just loved talking down to her like she was some nutcase, didn't he? "Cut the crap, Dad," she shouted. "What do you want? I'm sick of playing games. You want the money? Is that it?" She jammed her hand into her pocket. "I think I got five bucks in here some-where—"

"Eighty," he interrupted.

She paused. She could see that his jaw had suddenly become tightly set. "What?"

"Eighty dollars," he stated. "I can play that way, too, Lara. If you're going to pay me back, pay what you owe me. Pay me the money you stole from my register."

She blinked. Her insides twisted. She'd completely forgotten about that. "I—I . . ."

"While you're at it, you can also reimburse me for the liquor you took from the kitchen. The bill comes to about two hundred dollars."

Bile surged to the top of her throat. For a moment she felt as if she were going to vomit all over the car.

Mr. Passmore glanced at her. "Don't insult me anymore, Lara." His face darkened. "I've had enough. It's offensive."

"I—I . . . ," she stuttered again, but she had no idea what she was going to say. She gripped the side of the door until her nausea passed, unable to keep from staring at him.

His eyes flashed up at a sign above the highway. "Well, we're almost there," he mumbled. "I guess we can work the money issue out later, huh?" He moved the van into the exit lane.

Lara tore her eyes away from him. She'd never heard him talk like that—so cold and businesslike, so absolutely devoid of any emotion. It made her feel empty. But why should she even care? It wasn't as if he had ever really acted like her father in the first place. He'd given her a place to crash for a few months, a lame job, and that was about it. She should have been glad she was leaving him behind for a while.

"Do you even know that Benjamin got his sight back?" he suddenly demanded in the silence. His voice was harsh, accusing. "Do you?"

The question took her off guard. She shook her head, bewildered. Was he putting her on? "No," she answered quietly. "I had no idea. . . ."

"Yeah, well, he did," Mr. Passmore muttered in disgust. "He saw you last night, passed out on the living-room rug. You made quite a first impression."

She felt as if she had just been slapped. She shook her head.

"You never even thanked Zoey for cleaning up your mess!" he barked.

"I—I'm sorry."

He shrugged. "So you say, Lara. So you say. You're the girl who cried 'sorry.'" He spun the steering wheel, turning the van onto a pleasant, wooded two-lane road.

"Sometimes I mean it," she murmured. She knew she was on the verge of tears—but she couldn't help it. Why was he doing this to her?

"Maybe you do," he said hollowly.

"Just like you're so sorry for being such a crappy

father, for not even showing up for the first sixteen years of my life. Whoops! Sorry about that!"

Mr. Passmore bit his lip. His forehead suddenly flushed. "I've done my best, Lara," he said softly. "But I can't change the past."

The van climbed up a suddenly steep incline, then rounded a corner. A gate appeared before them with a plaque that read Serenity Hills Rehabilitation Clinic. Mr. Passmore slowed to a stop as a uniformed guard approached.

Lara tried to swallow, but her throat felt like sandpaper. This place had *guards?* She looked at the guy: He probably weighed at least two hundred pounds and had a nightstick. This was like prison. There was no difference.

"Can I help you?" the guard asked.

"Yes," Mr. Passmore said. "I have an appointment with Dr. Brower."

The guard gestured through the gate toward a red-brick building at the end of a long driveway. "You can park on the other side. Someone inside will show you to Dr. Brower's office." He headed back into his little guard booth. A moment later the gates began to swing open.

"It looks like a nice place," Mr. Passmore commented as he drove through the gates. "Very pretty."

Lara scanned the wide green lawns and carefully manicured shrubs, but her mind was squirming. *That's easy for you to say. You're not going to be trapped here.*

Her earlier sorrow rapidly faded. It was replaced with anger. She no longer felt like crying. At that very moment Lara knew she had to escape. Maybe not on the first day—maybe not even within the first week.

But she knew she would. And the first thing she would do would be to return to Chatham Island to teach the Passmore family a lesson. They weren't going to get away with locking her up. None of them were.

Least of all perfect little Zoey.

Somehow in the confusion of the party at Gray House, Zoey had lost Lucas.

She stood in the middle of the foyer floor, frowning. He must have gone upstairs. She glanced first into the dining room, then into the living room—but there was no sign of him. There were just a lot of people in suits milling around tables.

"Lucas?" she called, running up the stairs.

Claire suddenly turned the corner on her way down. "Have you seen Lucas?" Zoey asked.

"Yeah," Claire replied with a mischievous little smirk. She glanced over her shoulder as she continued down the steps. "He's looking lost. You better go get him before he . . . uh, wanders too far. Don't take too long up there—we're about to eat."

Zoey frowned. Lost? She hurried up to the second-floor landing. "Lucas?" she asked, looking both ways.

"Shhh!"

She turned to see Lucas poking his head around the corner to the right, his finger over his impishly grinning lips.

Her forehead wrinkled. "What are you—"

"Don't talk," he mouthed silently. He waved for her to follow, then disappeared back behind the wall.

Oh, great, Zoey thought, rolling her eyes. He was

probably using this opportunity to sneak up to an empty room while everyone was downstairs. Good old Lucas. At least he was reliable. You could always count on him for thinking about certain things at totally inappropriate times.

She rounded the corner to see him peeking through the cracked door of one of the guest rooms. He looked behind him and placed his fingers over his lips again—then gestured through the door.

What was he *doing?* Zoey tiptoed over to him and poked her head over his shoulder.

There, in the shadowy guest room, were Jake and Kate. They were rolling across the king-size bed, making out furiously.

Her eyes widened. All she could think was: Had Jake ever been that passionate with *her?* Just then Lucas yanked her back down the hall. His other hand was cupped over his mouth to keep from laughing.

In spite of herself Zoey was smiling, too. "Wow," she hissed. They paused by the top of the stairs. "I guess they worked things out."

When Lucas finally gained control of himself, he gave her a skeptical look. "And I wonder how that happened," he asked.

Zoey shook her head. "Lucas, I was going to tell you—"

"It's okay, it's okay," he said, taking her in his arms. "I know you can't keep a secret, Zo. It's something I've known for a long time. But you know what? I *still* love you. "

Zoey felt like she should protest, that she should be indignant . . . but she couldn't. Lucas was right. She couldn't keep a secret to save her life.

"And that dress you're wearing also helps put me

in a forgiving mood," he murmured huskily.

"You don't look so shabby yourself in that suit," she found herself saying, and the next thing she knew, she was kissing him. She couldn't believe she had actually been dreading the moment when she would have to confess that she'd told Jake about Lara. Funny how things worked out.

Finally she stepped away. "Lucas, I'm sorry I broke my promise to you," she breathed.

"It's okay. Really, Zo. I would have told Jake myself sooner or later, anyway." He grinned. "Or killed both of them."

She slapped him playfully on the chest. "We should probably go downstairs. I just saw Claire. . . ."

"I'll bet you did." He laughed. "Claire was the one who told me about what was going on up here."

"Oh." For some reason, Zoey blushed. Maybe it was just the thought of one person after another walking up and stealing a quick glimpse of what was going on in that back room.

"I think Jake and Kate had the right idea," Lucas whispered in Zoey's ear. He started kissing her neck.

"Lucas. . . ." She laughed and wriggled out of his grasp. "Come on, if everyone disappeared up here, that wouldn't be very polite, would it?"

He raised his eyebrows. "Since when have *I* ever worried about being polite?"

"Good point." She took his hand and began dragging him down the stairs. "But now's as good a time to start as any."

He followed reluctantly. "You really want to sit through a bunch of boring toasts?" he whispered.

"It's not a question of *want*," Zoey whispered back. "We have to."

They hurried into the living room, taking their places at a table with Benjamin, Mr. and Mrs. Passmore, the Cabrals . . . and an empty seat. Zoey looked at the place card: *Kate Levin.* Lucas snickered.

A hush fell over the room as Aaron walked into the foyer with a tall glass of champagne.

"Where's Kate?" Mr. Cabral whispered.

Zoey and Lucas shrugged simultaneously.

"Ladies and gentlemen!" Aaron's voice boomed out at them, echoing across the walls. "If I can have your attention, please. I'd just like to tell a little story." A wide smile broke on his face. "When my mother first mentioned the name Burke Geiger . . ."

Zoey immediately found herself zoning out. *Uh-oh.* Judging from the way Aaron loved to hear his own voice, this story was probably going to last about a half hour. What had she ever seen in him? She could hardly remember now. True, he was a talented musician—he had been dazzling the women of Chatham Island with his acoustic guitar for the past hour or so at the reception. And he was undeniably good looking, in a slimy kind of way. She glanced out of the corner of her eye at Lucas. Aaron could never compare to Lucas in a million years.

". . . and so I say to Burke Geiger and Sarah Mendel, *l'chaim!*" Aaron raised his glass. "To life!"

"To life!" everyone called in response.

"Now let's eat," he said.

There was laughter and the sound of chairs scuffling as everyone took their seats. All of a sudden Zoey heard Aisha's voice calling out over the crowd: "Wait a second, wait a second! I have an important announcement!"

She joined Aaron in the middle of the foyer and raised her own glass. "Sorry to steal the spotlight, but I couldn't resist."

Zoey shot a questioning look across the room at Nina. She wondered if Eesh was drunk. She *never* called attention to herself.

"I have a very important announcement," she repeated in the curious silence that followed. She raised her glass. "Christopher and I are engaged to be married!"

Zoey's eyes bulged. All at once there was complete pandemonium—all the women were rushing out of their chairs into the foyer and hugging Aisha, and all the men seemed to be flocking around Christopher. Besides Zoey the only people still sitting were Lucas and Nina.

And then Zoey started laughing.

"Hey, Zo?" Lucas whispered. "What's so funny?"

"I'm not sure. I think it's because I'm learning that all clichés really *are* true." She leaned over and kissed him. "You really *do* meet your future spouse at a wedding."

Making Out:
Kate finds love

Book 19 in the explosive series about broken hearts, secrets, friendship, and of course, love.

Jake and **Kate** are blissfully happy now that **Zoey's** told **Jake** the truth about **Lara**. **Kate** wants to spend every moment with **Jake,** so how can he tell her that he's heading for trouble unless she leaves him alone? The truth will hurt when ...

Kate
finds
love

READ ONE...READ THEM ALL—
The Hot New Series about Falling in Love

M A K I N G   O U T

by KATHERINE APPLEGATE

MAKING OUT

by KATHERINE APPLEGATE

Love stories just a little more perfect than real life...

Don't miss any in the

enchanted♥HEARTS
series: